GW00758799

VIRGIN LAND

CHLOE SMITH

LUNA NOVELLA #18

Luna Press PUBLISHING

Text Copyright © 2023 Chloe Smith
Cover © 2023 Jay Johnstone

First published by Luna Press Publishing, Edinburgh, 2023

The right of Chloe Smith to be identified as the Author of the Work has been asserted by her in accordance with the Copyright, Designs and Patents Act 1988.

Virgin Land ©2023. All rights reserved. No part of this publication may be reproduced, stored in a retrieval system, or transmitted in any form or by any means, electronic, mechanical, photocopy, recording or otherwise, without prior written permission of the copyright owners. Nor can it be circulated in any form of binding or cover other than that in which it is published and without similar condition including this condition being imposed on a subsequent purchaser.

www.lunapresspublishing.com
ISBN-13: 978-1-915556-03-5

For the teller of the snake story that began all this.
And for Emma, who retold it to me.

Contents

Chapter One

I'm leaving the greenhouse, arms full of harvested chard, skirt soiled with alien dirt and homemade water, when the shadow of a shikra passes over me and leaves me cold.

It takes a moment to understand what has happened. I peer up, confused, when the sunlight flickers and dims. My gut-formed thought, that it must be a ship, evaporates as soon as my reason catches up. There's no one on this side of the planet but Gerald and me. Remembering that fact makes my heart sink, even though I know it shouldn't.

Then I register the shape, and I forget my traitorous heart. Far up in the sky, the shadow is still terrifyingly large. I can make out spiky pinions and the sail-like stretch of webbing between them. Instinct makes me flinch and duck backwards, press myself against the greenhouse wall. Then the shadow is gone, beyond my range of sight.

I stay frozen for a long time, heart pounding. My eyes strain upwards, trying to pinpoint any movement in the vast, empty sky.

After I convince myself to move again, I go looking for Gerald. I try not to hunch under the open air as I move between the cluster of outbuildings.

He's not in the refrigerated storehouse, with its library of imported seeds and array of hoss embryos in their suspenta pods. Instead, I find him tinkering in the barn, next to the stall where our first litter of hosses squeaks and whuffles around, adapting to their new world better than I am. *They don't know about shikra yet.*

"What is it?" He frowns when he sees me.

"I saw a shikra." My voice comes out rough and unformed. I swallow and try again. "It passed overhead."

He lets his tools drop and stands up. "Are you sure?"

I bite back my first responses—*What else could it have been? Why can't you trust my judgement?* I settle on, "I saw its wings." I think back to the wall of the greenhouse at my back, the way the shape disappeared beyond the apex of my view. "It was headed northwest, I think."

"At high altitude? And it just passed by?" I nod and then nod again, and he sighs.

"I could do a perimeter run around the buildings, but for what, Shay? It's long gone, now, and probably running scared. How many shikra have we seen since you got here?" He catches himself, "And I don't mean the ones at the Erdehame compound."

I shiver at the thought of those carcasses, almost as long as I am tall, wings and limbs folded and tied tight together. The realisation that those bundles had been living things turned my stomach.

That image dominates my memory of my first visit to this planet's largest settlement. It was only a few weeks after Gerald fetched me here. Everything on Erde, from the ceilingless sky to the swarming reality of planetary life, was still so new, so overwhelming, that it shouldn't have stood out. But I froze in the middle of Erdehame, on the flat-packed dirt between the blocks of communal houses, and stared wordlessly until Gerald, who was talking to a Green Brigade soldier, finally noticed my distress and brought me away.

He thinks my pause now means I need clarification. "I meant a live shikra. How many have you seen *here*?"

He knows the answer, but I tell him anyway. "One."

"Yes, and I killed it, remember?" He takes my hand, squeezes it. "You keep an eye out, if you're nervous, but you won't see anything more. You're safe here, my love." He lets go, eyes drifting back to the disassembled feeder. "I need to finish reprogramming this."

I hesitate as he starts fiddling again. I tell myself he's right. I'm overreacting. Too fragile, too easily stunned, down here where air isn't rationed and gravity holds you in place. I'm still struggling to adjust to the way this world stretches beyond my perception, the way so many things grow without permission, without the careful rationing and tending that it takes to keep hydroponic gardens and protein vats productive.

Gerald gives me one last smile over his shoulder. "Dinner at the usual time?" It's a question, but also not. I nod, although he's not looking at me anymore.

I push myself to stand tall, strong enough to walk back out under the sky.

*

Nothing else passes overhead that day. My only encounters with irrepressible life are the two varieties of Small Things that I catch in the pantry. Something must have scraped or gnawed another hole in the house, somewhere. Gerald isn't as conscientious as I am about seal inspections. He's only lived a year more than I have outside of the environment bubbles that ships maintain, but it's as if that life never marked him. He's not bothered by the way the world constantly seeps inside.

At least the Small Things aren't bad. They're on the rodentlike end of the spectrum of creatures, mostly little burrowing quadrupeds and hexapods, that make their homes in the kudzu. The alien plant is even thicker and more profuse than its old-world namesake, and I don't know if Erde's original surveyors even identified all the creatures that hide in its undergrowth. In my ignorance, I've started giving them my own names. These two are both Slightly-Less-Cute Things. The 'Slightly Less' is because they seem to like human food almost as much as kudzu or whatever else they ate before we arrived.

I throw the two of them back into the kudzu and resolve to inspect all the house's potential entry points tomorrow. I could bring it up to Gerald—he always snorts at my naming practices, and as one of the few jokes we share it adds lubricant to the sticking points in our conversation—but I don't want it to seem like I'm criticising him.

When Gerald finally comes in, I expect him to follow up about the shikra, but he never even thinks to ask me how I'm feeling about it. Instead, after dinner, and after he insists that we sit outside on the porch to take in the sunset view, he waxes rhapsodic on his favourite topic.

When Gerald talks about his claim on Erde, his voice goes soft. Reverent. I can feel how much the idea draws at him, engrossing as a dream. He says, "It's virgin land, Shay. Unspoiled. All of this." He gestures, a full-armed movement, towards the wide horizon that circles us, as if his words mean anything after all these repetitions. As if they ever did.

Lamps in the house's—our house's—windows throw yellow stains onto the porch where we sit, but our faces are turned outward to the dusk. I nod, even though he can't see me, even though he's not looking. My habits of compliance are like my stays: a rigid and invisible support. They, too, sometimes make me wonder if I am smothering in the alien air—if, somehow, the survey team that rated Erde's atmosphere made some fatal error when they pronounced it benign for humans. Maybe it's some minor trace compound that makes my breath go high and tight in my throat….

No. No, that is ridiculous. I draw a breath in carefully, silently. through my nose. It smells as it always does at dusk, the lemony scent of the kudzu strong enough to mask any lingering cooking aromas, or even the smell of our own animal sweat from the day's work. Gerald has paused in his monologue, waiting for acknowledgement, and I make an encouraging noise. That's good enough for him to continue on.

"The shift I wrote into the feeder will get the hosses acclimated to local foliage, then, with the clear land, we can get started on the real work." I follow his gaze, past the dark lumps of buildings, out across the shadowed undulations of low hills. The kudzu's yellowy, twisting stems cover the land in a wild profusion that reaches higher than our heads. Even with all the times we've cut it back, the new growth still presses almost to the foot of this porch.

The scalloped silhouette of the porch's awning and its fluted columns make a black frame for the purple-gold sky, where light lingers even as the land beneath it grows darker. It's pretty, for once, caught between the scorching brilliance of the day and the lonely darkness of the night. That last is a misnomer: day and night are equally lonely here.

"Shay?"

I realise Gerald has turned to peer at me. I must have missed a cue to indicate agreement. "Oh…yes, definitely." I can make out his frown, and I add, "I'm sorry. I think I must be overtired," hoping that will mollify him.

He puts a hand on my knee. "Oh, Shay. You work so hard." For a moment, I feel the warmth of his solicitousness, the attention that softened him when he first courted me. "We all have to. It's the price of what we can achieve here." He turns back to the expanse of land.

I've lost him again. I say, "I think I should turn in, then."

He agrees. "We've got our work cut out for us tomorrow. The crew arrives early."

"Wait—who arrives early?" My mind goes back to the flurry of emotions when I saw the shikra, when I thought it was a ship.

"The crew to help clear the land—that's what I just told you. Weren't you listening?"

"Oh, yes. Of course." I don't know what I was expecting. Certainly not the familiar faces from home. That is an impossibility. It would have been nice to have more warning of strangers' arrival, though. This work crew is part of yet another plan Gerald made alone, assuming I would adapt. That's what I do.

I put my hand on his shoulder as I go in. It's strange that I still find comfort in his touch.

It's the same when he comes to bed. I fit neatly in the curl of his body, and I relish the warmth of his presence, even as I feel my anxious, lonely mind drifting farther and farther from the rock of his certainty.

I try to leech belief from him the way I leech body heat, and I lie still, listening to the creak of the house in the alien wind, the chirps and other unfamiliar sounds. Things move among the thickets of kudzu that cover the rolling hills in all directions.

*

My father felt the pull of virgin land as well. He told all his children that we would be settlers, that we should work towards the opportunity to start fresh on untouched soil. Despite his hopes, I was born on the *Beyond*, a prospecting ship whose grappling arms wrenched chunks of ore from frozen planetoids and threshed comet tails for their icy harvests. In Papa's view, that unforgiving work was the next best thing to true settler life. He didn't want a landscape that someone else had softened with their presence—no regulations, no communities, no growing populations whose appetites would suck a world's resources dry.

"Most people are takers," he'd tell us. "Even when they don't work for Astra, Hyun-Raum, or any of the other corporations. No—it's human nature. Inescapable truth. The only hope is to find a place they haven't started picking away at yet."

I didn't doubt him. There were the vids he'd shown me, of the ravaged Earth, its plastic-swamped oceans and blasted plains. I'd witnessed the greed and surliness of people when they came together, in the fetid, rusty bellies of the trading stations. I have an early memory of following in my father's footsteps through a station's narrow corridor, all of us children holding hands and pressed together as we hurried, assaulted on all sides by smells and noises, soliciting voices and hands reaching to pull on our shirtsleeves. The confusion of that moment distilled and hardened in my memory, an explanation for the distaste in Papa's voice when he talked about outsiders and their stations, the picked-over planets, the massive companies whose only ethic was profit. I didn't wonder why, if that was the corruption we'd have to wade through, we visited them so rarely, kept to our own ship and the isolation of the asteroid fields, our only regular contacts with like-minded settler folk.

Papa brought Gerald home as a fellow traveller, a family friend before he ever met me. He and my father had made a rare connection in one of those squalid depot stations, discovered that they shared the settler values and the settler dream. Like Papa, Gerald was biding his time with prospecting work, trading raw asteroid innards by the ton for micrograms of profit. We all marvelled when my father introduced a stranger, telling us that this man would pool his efforts with ours for a few hauls, to everybody's benefit. It didn't take long for Gerald to win us all over, though, with his fierce eyes full of distant visions.

My littlest siblings goggled at his stories of travel across the surfaces of habitable planets; my age-mate Julia blushed up to her eyes every time he looked at her; and my two oldest brothers, Cai and Jem, took his presence as a direct model for how to be and act. I was as lost as the rest, and flattered, besides, at the attention he paid me. He was poised on the edge of greatness, we all could tell. He wouldn't be held back by all the obstacles to settler dreams.

"Either they'll let anyone down the gravity well," Papa would complain, sitting astride a bench in the *Beyond*'s galley as Julia and I prepared dinner, "or else the whole thing is tied up in surveys and regulations for generations. Creakin' Cygni. Far be it for them to trust us, the people best suited to make use of all that unspoiled land."

Gerald, seated across from him, would agree that it was unfair. Despite the swarm of competing polities—merchant fleets, sovereign nations, corporate entities, collective societies, and more—scattered across the depths of space, the Cygni Authority had a stranglehold on the long-leap technology that drove frontier exploration.

I was used to hearing Papa curse Cygni and their rules. They might be one step above the mining and resource-harvesting companies like Hyun-Ruam, the top predators of station and colony societies, but they didn't hold to settler ethics, either. Papa hated the way they would either throw the doors wide and encourage *anyone* to move to new planets (usually the least livable, where humans would have to huddle and glom together to survive), or else identify the worlds as sentient-populated and so closed to any settlement. (Those were usually the richest, most promising planets, too. Papa always snorted at the idea of some creepy crawly or monstrous lizard whose "questionable ability to pattern back at us" meant that they must be using all the space they had down there).

The hope that all would-be settlers cling to is to make it onto one of the private worlds. Sometimes—and when Papa got going on the specifics of how and when, there was so much huffing and imprecating that I inevitably tuned out the complicated details—Cygni released control of newly surveyed planets to a single polity or org. And even rarer than that 'sometimes,' the org was a pro-settler one, like the Green Brigade.

Gerald was always optimistic about the Green Brigade, always certain they would answer his hopes. He'd even defend their practices when Papa groused about their exorbitant claim prices.

"Everyone wants their piece." Papa sipped the mug of vatbeer I'd pulled for him and made a face. "The Brigade talks a good talk, but do they really act with the hearts of settlers? No, they're takers. Too far from real, human work, from the way we could be, if we had freedom and plenty."

"It's a taker's universe," Gerald agreed. It was a truism of dissatisfaction I'd heard often enough. But then he added, "The Brigade does what they can to make settler worlds a reality, though. How would they pay for their operations, if they didn't realise profit from the land? They have to support themselves somehow."

"So says the bright-eyed young man." Papa's smile didn't hide the bitterness in his tone.

"I can't help my optimism. It's the example of dedicated folks like you and yours." Gerald lifted his own mug in toast, "You inspire me." He spoke to Papa, but his eyes sought mine.

I remember the flash of possibility that went through me then. That moment, I felt as if a hatch had opened on a new and impossible vista, suggesting a path I'd hardly believed would ever actually be mine. Gerald's smile, the promise of his words to my father, stay clear and perfect in my mind, however far away they seem now.

That possibility seemed even brighter when Gerald announced, on his next visit, that he'd secured a land claim on a newly opened world called Erde. It created a glow of anticipation that made all my other memories of that time blurry and dreamlike. The pounding of my heart muffled the sound my father's perplexed questions—how had Gerald managed to afford such a claim? Where was he selling his rock hauls at those rates? I don't remember the words Gerald used to soothe Papa, nor yet the details of his urgent, enthusiastic proposal of marriage to me.

He told me that he would send for me when he was settled. Papa, even confused and jealous of Gerald, admitted that was a golden opportunity. I was certain I agreed. The months I spent waiting for Gerald's summons stretched and seemed interminable. It was the only time I ever felt cramped in my family's ship, maddened by the chatter of the littles, by my father's lectures, by the way Cai always had to have the last word or Julia snorted through her nose when she laughed.

What I wouldn't give to hear her snort now, or to have Cai contradict me. I don't know if I would have any more patience for Papa's words, though. I hear them now in Gerald's voice.

*

I wake up before the alarm and dress myself in the dark. I'm almost used to the awkwardness of tightening my own stays, the absence of my sisters' hands. I hesitate before I head to the kitchen, remembering Gerald's words about adjusting the feeder. Will he remember to check on the hosses before beginning the day's main work? Easier to do it myself. The grey predawn sky is still empty as I hurry across to the barn.

This building, at least, has tight seals. Gerald is careful to keep the imported livestock insulated as they adjust to this planet's air, water, and bacteria. Inside the barn, panels of flexible, near-transparent shielding hang in overlapping folds around the stall that holds our firstborn litter. Inside, the creatures are mostly quiet, although a few stagger around on their little long-toed feet. The teats of the automated feeder jut from the far wall, and while none of the hosses are currently suckling, a couple lie beneath it, sides rising and falling in what looks like contented sleep.

Gerald explained to me that hosses are neospecies built from the genetic inheritance of antique ruminants and rodents—"the best of cow, goat, and capybara," he said, and I nodded at the memory of pictures from the *Beyond*'s data library. For all my father's settler ideals, I never saw an animal, much less took care of one, before Erde. Gerald is confident in his purchased embryo stock, though, so I try to be as well.

I'm still not sure what thriving looks like, but the vitals readout next to the stall isn't throwing out any alerts, so I dismiss that worry from today's list.

The next to-do is breakfast. For all that I hate the omnipresent kudzu, the way it clogs the landscape and pushes constantly against itself, against other plants, against anything we build, I have to admit it has its positive qualities. Even alien plants on strange worlds grow reserves of starchy carbohydrates in their roots and stems, it turns out. Kudzu is nutritious—if not delightful—for humans, once it's been treated to leach away the toxins. Bread stuffs made from ground kudzu root form the foundation of our diet here, although I'm still trying out different ways to make it less insipid.

I'm stewing mash when Gerald speaks from the doorway. "It's too bad these off-worlders likely won't appreciate the luxury of a homecooked meal, made with the fruits of our own land."

I'm so surprised I turn towards him. "What off-worlders?"

"The ones I hired. Really, Shay. How many times do I have to tell you?"

I really should have paid more attention. It's hard, though, when his words flow over me every day, not to begin walling myself away from them. I try to brush past the moment with another question. "None of the neighbours would agree to help?"

Neighbours is a generous term; there are still only a scattering of people on this planet, and the nearest are hours of flight away, beyond the border of Gerald's immense claim. I would have thought they'd still come, though. Papa always liked to point out that, away from the corruption of crowded living, people didn't forget their human duty to help each other. Settlers believe in community and mutual support.

Gerald shrugs, which makes me wonder whether he even asked any of them. "You're dripping water on the floor, and the tap is running. Don't waste it."

I turn towards the cooking surface again and let a retort fizzle silent on my tongue. Our water recycling is tight and efficient. I make sure of it. If he is so chary of waste, why did he hire off-worlders who will take their pay out of his savings rather than expecting future help in kind?

Gerald doesn't say anything more, but I hear him moving around. When I look back, I find he's pulled packages of shelf-stable protein slabs out of a cupboard and taken up one of the knives to cut portions. I blink. Cooking is my job, and he only gestures towards helping with it when he suspects he's been unreasonable. That doesn't happen as often as it should.

His help never lasts that long, either. He brings out chives and mushrooms next, but before I can ask him to chop them as well, he changes direction and heads for the door, leaving me to continue on my own.

I almost speak to his departing back. *If you can reach off-world and contact strangers so easily, why do I have to wait months for a visit to the comm station and a single letter from home?* The question catches like a grappling hook in my throat and drags as I swallow it down. Gerald surely has his own preparations to make for the day, and I don't have the energy to batter against his stonewalling.

I let the work of cooking become its own distraction as the sky lightens. It's comforting to prepare for more than two mouths. I can almost imagine myself back in the galley of the *Beyond*.

The shuttle arrives with a roar so low my ears hum with it. When I hear boots echoing on the boards of the porch, my heart quickens. It's not the same sound as my siblings clambering through an access hatch, but it makes me think of their eager crowding nonetheless.

I leave my apron on a chair back before venturing outside. Gerald is holding forth, explaining his plans for the land and the advantages of the hoss strain: "…developed on Calle III, but they will thrive on this world…." He catches sight of me and reins himself in, "But I've let my enthusiasm distract me from the practicalities. Here is my wife, who has prepared breakfast for us."

The work crew turns to me. Three men and a woman, I would guess, although I don't always recognise gender markers among outsiders. For one thing, their clothing is a far cry from the formal rigid bodices and tailored vests that distinguish settler folk: they are all dressed alike in belted coveralls. It's a practical concession to life without a planet's reliable gravity. At home, onboard the *Beyond*, even I and the other women and girls wore trousers. My skirts now are a badge of success— of settler life as it's supposed to be lived. I realise that I've started brushing them straight with my hands and do my best to stand still as I look back at the outsiders.

Four pairs of eyes are not a lot, but it's still more observation than I've felt in months, and my face heats. Gerald raises his eyebrows, prompting.

"You're welcome to come in, and I hope you will eat with us…." I hesitate, then finish in a rush, "A long day of work will feel longer if you aren't fed beforehand."

*

I wish I hadn't spent so much time thinking of family this morning. Of course it's not like that when we sit down. Gerald's voice still fills the air. I pass the dishes. The crew, none of whom Gerald has bothered to introduce, nod and dig into their food without hesitation. They stay almost as quiet as I do, letting Gerald fill the air with explanations about the greenhouse, the ranch, the work he did to build this place of his.

This place of ours, I remind myself.

"I was the first man to walk this stretch of terrain," Gerald says. "It's a dream come true that we should be the heirs to an unspoiled paradise like this."

"Unspoiled?" One of the men sits up straighter, tone still friendly, but sharper than the polite murmurs they've all been dropping into Gerald's pauses. "So what did Green Brigade do when they came through and shot the local megafauna out of the sky?"

The other two men tense, and their eyes go from their companion to Gerald. My hand cramps around my spoon. I can feel the outburst coming.

Gerald barks, "What's that supposed to mean? People are

trying to live here, to build homes and families. The shikra were a monstrous menace."

The spacer shrugs. He's a big man, and he leans forward on his elbows. I think of the crowding in the station corridors. "It just seems odd to call a place untouched when an armed group practically exterminated a species before you got here. And you're their heir? Does that make the Green Brigade the midwives, welcoming you into this new life? Or are they the lawyers, putting a stamp of legitimacy on your division of this planet's spoils?"

"I'm sure I don't know what you mean, talking about legitimacy, spoils." Gerald keeps bearing down. "And anyway, who are you to ask about us, or the shikra, or anything the Green Brigade does? You don't know what it means to be a settler."

"Maybe not—" The big spacer begins, but then jerks, catches himself, and glares at his immediate neighbor, as if the other man just kicked him under the table.

The female spacer puts down her spoon with a clink in the sudden silence, and says, "Luca. Enough."

The big man, Luca, withers under her gaze. "Yes, Captain."

This is the crew's captain? She's a broad-shouldered woman, although not as big as Luca, with wide-set eyes above sharp cheekbones and a decisive chin. She has surprisingly delicate hands, which she laces in front of her as she speaks to Gerald.

"Settler Gainrad, I apologise. Luca spoke out of turn, from an abundance of passion. His training is in field biology, so he naturally has a lot of feelings—but he can and should divorce his personal interests from the task at hand." She keeps her gaze on Gerald, expression neutral, but her tone is adamantine, unyielding. Her crew members shift in their seats.

Gerald huffs. "I hired you for labour, not for any ill-formed opinions on land management."

"Of course," the woman agrees. "Travelling crews like ours have to take the work we find, whatever our original vocation. We do what we can." She inclines her head.

I'm fascinated by this woman's presence. The way she holds herself, the banked authority that, even while she's apologising, holds no hint of subservience. I can't understand, now, how I didn't see immediately that she is their leader.

"I should think so," Gerald says, chasing back to his original source of outrage. "And you should know, Captain Tinsdale, that everything the Green Brigade has done here is to assure our safety. And why shouldn't they? The odds of finding a planet like this—rich and compatible with human life, full of resources that we can use, and use right this time. It's like it was made for us."

None of the spacers respond to that. The captain—Tinsdale—waits a beat, as if examining some unspoken thought, then returns to her breakfast. I look down at my own plate. The kudzu mash—an acquired taste at the best of times—is cottony in my mouth.

At last Gerald pushes his chair back. "Daylight's wasting. Time to get started. If that's not objectionable to you?" The scorn in his voice makes me wince.

Tinsdale seems not to notice. "We're here for the job." She stands as well, and her crew along with her. Then she turns to look down at me. "Thank you for the meal." She doesn't smile, but her eyes soften a fraction. They are big and dark as the outer void. I duck my head, self-conscious.

*

Gerald stops before I can follow them outside. "We won't break for food again until evening. You should stay here. Take care of things in the house."

"Really?" I ask him. The clearing work, even with extra hands and our two groundcraft, will be a mighty labour. I had assumed it would be like anything else that has to get done here: Gerald counting on my help.

Instead, his stiff form fills the doorway. "I wouldn't ask you to leave the sphere of our home." The tension of his posture is like a finger pointing at these outsiders.

Why does Gerald need this pretence? Does he want me like the land, unspoiled by further contact? I thought I'd be done with confinement when I left the Beyond.

The argument, the obvious points, crowd the back of my throat. Gerald shifts and frowns. His figure blocks the light from the open door.

I tell myself it's not important. It's just a few days, and it's easier, in the long run, to keep Gerald happy—when your entire life encompasses only one other person, the thing that matters is erasing the points of friction.

I swallow my thoughts down again. "Alright. But let me know if you realise you need another driver."

"You're sweet to offer, Shay." He smiles and is gone.

When we first moved to this alien world, I thought his praise would fill the hollow inside me, but it just chafes at the edges.

Outside, I can hear the noise of work starting—the hum and purr of the groundcraft; raised voices; the rustle and occasional crack and thump of felled and uprooted kudzu. Around me, the house feels swathed in silence, its emptiness an echoing shell. My feet stutter-step towards the window before I stop myself. I won't be a face in the window, staring out at those distant strangers. Watching would only make me feel even more how alone I am.

Instead, I turn my back and head down to the house's basement to look for seal breaks, any small holes an alien lifeform could squeeze through. I should be able to find satisfaction in my labour: needed, supportive, reliable. A contribution to the larger work of settlement, however small. If only it didn't feel so much like battling alone against Erde's encroachments.

Chapter Two

My search for unauthorised entry points for small invaders lasts until I give up and turn to regular housework. Busy inside, I don't see the shadow that erupts from a mass of kudzu, or hear the screams that follow.

I've got my arms full of clean bed linens when I hear the front door slam and the thump of spacer boots again.

"Settler Gainrad!"

I think that they're calling for Gerald, that he came back early and is somewhere inside. I'm so startled I don't even put my burden down, just follow the sound to the front parlour.

Tinsdale and Luca hold Gerald between them. His feet skim the floor and his head lolls. A red-black stain spreads down his torso from behind a balled knot of cloth. He's holding it himself, but Tinsdale grips his wrist, keeping the material in place.

I should do something, say something. Instead, I stand there, holding my laundry in a death grip, as Luca takes Gerald's full weight, his large hands careful, and lowers my husband onto the couch. It's of a style with the rest of this ridiculous, overdecorated house, with an asymmetrical curving back and buttons punctuating the domes of its upholstery.

Gerald called it a fainting couch. I can't believe that this is what I'm thinking about right now.

Tinsdale looks up at me. She has a smear of blood down the side of her face. "Where's your automed?"

I look around, like a fool, before I catch myself and hurry forward. "We don't have one. Here." I thrust the sheets at her.

Her eyes widen. "What? Why would…" She grabs a sheet, presses it to the wound on Gerald's chest. Without releasing her hold, she barks, "Get to the shuttle. Pull an emergency pack." The other crewmember turns on his heel, then her attention is back on me. "Get whatever you do have, then."

The house threatens to spin around me as I run through it, my heart loud in my ears. I throw open the storage cabinet that holds our carefully hoarded medical supplies. I scoop up everything I can reach—coagulant bandages, antibiotic packs, antiseptics, painkillers. I could have gone for this as soon as I saw them. I could have been watching so I'd be prepared when they got here. I could have—

When I get back, the balled sheets are already lurid with Gerald's blood. Tinsdale's hands are gory. "Alright. Let's see what we can do." Her dark eyes take me in. "Can you help?"

I suck in air, forcing my mind clear. "Yes." I can do what needs to be done. I always do.

I know how to treat injuries, how to respond to the accidents that are inevitable both planetside and on shipboard. Once I'm involved, my own hands applying pressure, wiping clean, packing on the bandaging, I don't need to keep telling myself to breathe. We've got the bandage sealed by the time Luca returns with the portable emergency kit. It includes a diagnostic scanner, which Tinsdale affixes to the other side of Gerald's chest.

Tinsdale frowns down as it starts to spit out readings, then her posture sags a bit. I realise I'm not the only one who's been holding fear at bay. "It missed his lung," she says. "And there's no fracturing to his skull. The femur is a clean break."

I glance, then look again at Gerald's lower half. I hadn't even taken in in the contorted shape of one leg. Luca snorts at my double take, and Tinsdale glares at him.

"Apologies, Settler. If you like, I can…" I realise he's speaking to me, offering to step in. Tinsdale is placing careful hands on Gerald's twisted limb.

"We need to splint it," she tells me. "It'll take strength."

I stiffen. "Tell me what to do." Who is she to tell me I'm not strong enough?

"Okay." Her voice is gentle. Some part of me notes that she didn't mean to disparage me, but I can't reach rationality or calm. Instead, I simply hold myself tighter.

She shows me where to put my hands, and I hold the meat of Gerald's thigh so tightly I feel the scrape and shift of bone moving against bone as she straightens the leg. He yelps, wordlessly, but doesn't wake. I help lay another bandage against his skin, this one with a stiffening agent that will encase the limb. I arrange his limbs on the couch, cover him with a blanket. His face is grey and slack.

Tinsdale is saying something else, about rest and medicine. I try to make sense of her words, in time to catch the last of them: "…think he'll be fine."

I look up at her. "What happened?"

Tinsdale and Luca share a look, and she opens her mouth. "It was—"

The front door bangs open again. "Shikra got away, Captain." It's the other two members of Tinsdale's group.

The man who spoke is holding a long-barrelled weapon with a telescopic sight. "It's over the horizon now, moving on a north-northwest vector." He gestures with his chin at Gerald's still form. "What's Gainrad's status? He gonna live?"

Tinsdale makes a wordless noise of irritation. "Sayre. Show some sensitivity—" She's clearly tipping her head in my direction.

I cut her off. "We think that my husband, Settler Gainrad, will be fine." I clasp my hands in front of me, pretend they're not blood-smeared. "Thank you for your concern."

I swallow. I'm alone with outsiders. I have to speak to them, to hold them off, without Gerald or my father or anyone else to stand between me and the world of takers. "Don't think, simply because of this…this accident, you can shrug off your agreement with him. I—I will see that you complete the work you owe us."

I stare at Tinsdale, willing her not to laugh, not to kill me, not to turn and leave me alone on this horrible world, empty but for monsters that aren't all dead after all. I feel made from rust and weeds.

She starts to say something, hesitates. Finally, she says, "Of course we will honour our agreement. The work may take a few days longer without your husband's help, but we'll get it done."

"I won't count that against you." I hope I sound as hardnosed as any of the depot men my father had to trade with.

Her expression doesn't shift. She only says mildly, "That's good of you, Settler."

I glance down at Gerald. Somehow, I still expect him to speak up, to take charge of the situation. His face is still, though.

Tinsdale says, "Would you…like one of us to stay with you?"

"No!" Surprise makes the refusal more vehement than I meant it to. "I mean, no thank you. I can care for his needs. I don't want to leave you more shorthanded."

"Alright then. You have the emergency kit. There are hydration packets you can use, and the scanner will tell you if anything shifts, but he should be stable. Come find us if you need anything." She looks around at her crew, who've been watching us silently. "Let's get back to it, then."

They're almost all out the door when one question breaks through my façade of control. "What about the shikra? What will you do?"

The man with the weapon, Sayre, is bringing up the rear. He looks back at me. "Don't worry, ma'am. We were surprised, is all. If it comes near again, we'll be forewarned."

I try to find comfort in his words.

*

Before the day is over, I end up not just at the window, but standing out on the porch. I check on the hosses again. The formula levels in the feeder are still good, and they tumble over each other, full of energy. I balk at the idea of wading in to clean excrement out of their stall. There's plenty I could be doing in the house, but dinner is all but done and every time I try attend to other, less urgent tasks, I lose concentration, my ears straining for the sounds of another calamity. I keep interrupting myself to go check on Gerald. He came half-awake, groaning and muttering, halfway through the afternoon. I gave him water and medicine for the pain, and he subsided back into something like sleep. I don't know what more I can do. On the porch, at least, I'm distracted.

I shade my eyes and watch the outsiders work. A land-work groundcraft isn't a shuttle or a mining mech—and it took me weeks, when I arrived, to learn to handle our two craft with ease. The crew doesn't seem to be having difficulties, though.

Beyond the hollow where their shuttle crouches, I can see a wide and growing stretch of earth scattered with broken branches and oozing stumps. I wonder if they've done work like this before, in places where humans spread and multiply and take everything they can from the land and from each other. I don't know how Gerald found them, or what jobs itinerant spacers usually do. Anything they can? I think about Luca's strange accusations at breakfast, the easy way Sayre held his weapon, the shadow of the shikra in the sky. I feel the breath begin to go hard in my throat.

Raised voices come to me faintly across the distance. A figure stands up from the passenger seat of one of the groundcraft, gesticulating with both arms. It's Captain Tinsdale. The spacer driving the other craft stops, yells something in response, then bumps a few metres in reverse. They all climb down to inspect something on the ground—maybe a recalcitrant trunk or root system? It looks exactly like the labour Tinsdale promised. I think of her voice saying, "we will honour our agreement."

*

They stop in the late afternoon and disappear into their shuttle. I would have offered them the use of our washroom, imagining that they would prefer its space to whatever cramped facilities they have aboard, but they all reappear quickly, in clean coveralls with fresh hair and faces. Of course they must have a sonic shower onboard. I feel ashamed of my own loose tendrils and damp armpits. *They're takers*, I remind myself. *It shouldn't matter what they think of you.* They have to rely on those technologies because their societies have burned through everything that's good and natural.

"How is your husband?" Tinsdale asks me.

I feel a flash of guilty resentment. I should be sitting, loyal and caring, by his side. I open the door and lead them all inside again. "As you see. He seems to be resting quietly, at least."

Tinsdale goes over to the couch and inspects her scanner. The hiss of her indrawn breath jolts me back into the panic of the morning.

"Luca," Tinsdale says, "look at these readings."

"What?" I ask. Neither of them respond, and I can't stop myself from repeating, like a child, "What?"

Tinsdale and her crewman share a look before she finally turns back to me. "It seems the damage to his head was more severe than we thought. The scanner's a rough tool and, well, there could be swelling, or blood pooling. If you had an automed…" She shakes her head.

The fear and guilt coagulate into stinging anger. "Well, we don't," I snap. "We don't have a sonic shower, or a carbon recycler, or a med system that also juggles and sharpens our knives. It's just us out here, and whatever he chose to bring—" I catch myself, "whatever we could bring with us."

"Well, you didn't bring what you need now. Honestly, we wouldn't have taken a job like this if we knew there was no onsite med support. We have facilities onboard for emergency stasis, but nothing more. We can't fix him." Tinsdale has pulled herself up, tight and stiff, edging closer to confrontational.

"And, unless you want to try self-taught trepanning, neither do you. This is the point where we," she jerks her head towards the rest of her crew, "would be evacuating to the nearest treatment facility. Did you have any plan for medical emergencies, beyond blind optimism?"

I want to lash out at her, to scream that the plans were never mine, that I didn't have a choice—but even in this extremis, I can't pretend. I did choose. I take a breath, forcing myself, if not calm, at least to a rigidity that matches hers. Forcing myself to be reasonable, resourceful.

"The largest settlement on this planet is a multi-family claim. Erdehame compound. That's where the comm station is." I think back to our last supply run, trying to remember the configuration of the buildings. "They've a medical facility too."

"How far is it?" Luca asks.

"It's on the far continent. A day away by shuttlecraft."

"Ours can get you there in six hours," Tinsdale says. "I think we should try to wake him. His body could fall even farther asleep."

I'm suddenly terrified that Gerald's breathing could falter and cease while I'm not watching. I stare down at him, trying to make out the rise and fall of his chest. I'm afraid I'll hurt him more if I touch him. Luca is the one who tries first, gently, then with more noise and effort. "Settler Gainrad," he calls. His fingertips dig divots into Gerald's uninjured shoulder.

"Wha…? Urgh…" Gerald shifts and winces. His eyes crack open. I drop to my knees beside him.

"Gerald, we need to get you care for your injuries." He blinks at me. The pupils of his eyes are enormous. "These people, Captain Tinsdale and her crew, they've offered to take us to the Claim One settlement to get medical help."

"What? No!" His response it so sudden, so harsh, that it makes me jump, even as he jerks back as well, as if we've discovered another lurking creature between us. "We won't leave the land! It's ours. Erdehame, they don't understand.... They know…"

"Gerald," I plead, "You're confused. Please let us help you."

His gaze shifts to the crew, who stand around his couch. "The takers. We made an agreement."

"Settler Gainrad," Tinsdale says, "You have a head injury that's putting pressure on your brain. You need more help than we can provide here. Please listen to your wife."

He struggles to sit up. "Once we're away and on your ship, takers take what they want, do what they like. No. I won't abandon what's mine."

I feel the world tip sideways. I know Gerald's passion, his devotion to our claim, but this is irrational. I have to make him understand. "Please," I say, reaching out. "Gerald, you need things we don't have here. We need to go with them."

"No." He glares at me. "We must keep our presence here. We can't let other hands spoil it."

"They won't be here," I try. "Captain Tinsdale and her crew will be transporting us."

"I have to stay." He starts to shake his head, winces. "My agreement."

I close my eyes. How can I get through to him? I suck in a breath. "You need to go get care. One of the crew members will take you. I'll stay. I'll make sure the land gets cleared."

"That's not—" He tries again to struggle upward and comes up against the injuries to his leg and chest. He makes another involuntary noise, and I clutch at him in response.

"Please, Gerald! You need care. You need more than we have here…" I can feel tears pressing behind my eyes and hear them in my voice.

Maybe he hears them too, because his gaze focuses on me, "Don't cry, Shay."

I try to do as he says, but my reserves of iron are failing me. "Please…" the word comes out a hiccup. He can't die and leave me alone here. "Go get help, Gerald."

There's movement, and Luca and Sayre swoop in to lift Gerald between them. He doesn't try to fight them, at least, and somehow they get him to the hatch of their ship. I follow, and board behind them, hold his hand while Sayre straps him into one of the couches in the first cabin we come to.

I can hear Tinsdale giving her crew directions, and part of me wonders if maybe Gerald was right, and they are going to kidnap us, fly away to some dismal station and trade our organs for universal credits, sell this claim to some other wide-eyed, idealistic settler couple…

Then she is next to me, whispering in my ear. "Brain injuries can make people confused. I'm sure your husband wouldn't insist that you stay if he were in full control of his faculties. We could easily take you both."

I stiffen. "No, thank you. The plan we agreed on will be best." I turn to give her a look, to show how determined, how controlled I am, but I'm caught when I realise, for once, that I can read the expression in her eyes. It's sympathy.

Gerald pulls on my hand. "Shay? Where are we going? Who are these people?"

My stomach jumps. "These are the workers you hired to clear the land."

"I'm your taxi driver," Sayre says behind us. "We're going to pop around to the other hemisphere to get your medical needs sorted." I turn to look up at him, and he taps the shipboard headset he's donned. "I'll be keeping tabs on Settler Gainrad the whole way there, make sure he's stable and isn't in more pain. Don't worry, ma'am."

I smile, because that's a ridiculous thing to ask of me, and Sayre smiles back and nods. I squeeze Gerald's hand again, step away before he can think of any more objections and follow the others back off the ship.

We stand together in front of the house and watch as Sayre lifts the craft from the ground. It doesn't seem large anymore, and it shrinks so quickly into just another glowing dot in the evening sky that I suffer a sudden rush of vertigo at the emptiness in its place.

*

Dinner is a far quieter affair than breakfast was. I finally gather my courage to break through the echoing absence of Gerald's voice. "How did it happen?"

Tinsdale sighs and says, "The shikra was roosting in one of the largest kudzu on the far side of this house. We think it might have spent the night there, then seen our shuttle land and registered it as threat, been too frightened to leave. Your husband didn't realise it was there, went in to tie the trunk for hauling. They must have caught each other off guard."

My spine tightens at the idea. Was it the same shadow that passed me overhead? I can well imagine it exploding out of the foliage, all spiny limbs and expanding wings. I shudder.

"We've been careful since then, Settler," Tinsdale says, "We've worked out a system for checking the largest stands of growth, and of course mowing eliminates the places they could hide."

"And what's the population of shikra left on this planet now?" Luca adds, "What are the odds another will show up nearby?"

Tinsdale shoots him another look. "Those aren't the questions we're asking right now."

I try again, before the conversation can decay completely. "Why do you call me 'Settler'?"

This surprises them. "It's who you are, isn't it?" Tinsdale asks.

"We're settlers, but that's not my title. Properly speaking, that's my husband. He's the one who secured the land grant." I catch myself. They don't need my story.

Tinsdale only asks, "How should we address you, then?"

I consider. Goodwife was what my mother used, the rare times she spoke to anyone outside the family. Sayre's ma'am felt non-threatening. Those terms are likely what Gerald would prefer, if they have to address me at all.

"You can call me Shayla," I say. "That's my name."

Tinsdale gives me a long, opaque look. Her eyes are large and beautiful. "I'm Alis."

At the end of the meal, Sono, the small, wiry fourth crew member, hops up and begins stacking plates.

"You don't have to do that!" I tell him.

He smiles and ignores my objections. "Cooperative effort means it'll be done sooner, and we can all get our rest."

Rest. I hadn't even thought about where they would sleep. Their bunks are halfway to the comm station by now. I'm momentarily grateful for Gerald's confusion, that it prevented him from considering one more consequence of this plan—

that I would spend the night alone with these outsiders. I should be objecting as well, but I can only feel relief. My imagination curls away from the idea of trying to sleep in an empty house. I say, "We have spare bedrooms I can make up."

'Spare' in this case means waiting for children to fill them, as soon as the labour of establishing the hoss herds is behind us. It's another expectation Gerald built on when he chose the shape of this house, one that I can't think about too much. Its flavour of twinned hope and fear is too overwhelming. I add, "I'm afraid you'll have to share, as there are only two."

Tinsdale nods. "No problem there. Sono and Luca share a bunk most of the time."

I feel myself blush, and Tinsdale's mouth hardens. I wonder if she's expecting some ignorant outburst from me, some settler prejudice. I lift my chin. Just because settlers marry man-to-woman doesn't mean we know nothing else. The universe is wide, and I'm not ignorant. "I'll just go lay out bedding, then."

*

I wake suddenly, with a disorienting wrench, from a sleep so deep it had a gravitational pull. I register the feeling of empty space in the bed, and its wrongness, before I remember that it's Gerald I'm missing, before I remember what happened to him. I spend a half dozen breaths sitting up, arms wrapped around my knees, as I reaccustom myself to the strain and fear of the last day's reality.

It must be close to dawn. The air in the room has taken on a blue-grey tinge. I stare through it, wondering if there's any use in lying back down, pretending I can sleep for another hour. Instead, I unwrap myself from the blanket and swing my legs over the edge of the bed.

That's when I step on the snake.

I register its shivering movement beneath my bare foot before I feel any pain. I scramble back onto the bed with an inhaled shriek and hit the wall panel that controls the hanging cascade of lamp bulbs. On my knees now, I lean forward and stare down at it, heart pounding.

It's a small one, and it coils away across the floor with the strange, looping wriggle of a helix made of water.

I reach blindly for something, anything that will serve as a weapon. My hand finds a heavy weight on the nearest sidetable—a faceted polycrystal bowl that Gerald thought would charm me. I grip it between my fists and try my best to leap from the bed without taking my eyes from the snake. They can slither away too fast to follow, if you let them.

It coils tighter at my approach, and I hesitate, trying to gauge its readiness to attack. Its loops loosen—it's a small one, as snakes go, and it may be more ready to flee than strike at me. Before I can think further, I heft the bowl, and half-fall forward, bringing the weight down on the snake's body.

Erde's snakes are hardy creatures, for all their fluidity of movement. There's a crunch between the bowl and the floor. The section of the body I can still see shivers and then relaxes its curl. I relax, too, and rest, panting on the floor next to it as my adrenalin ebbs.

There's a knock at the door. "Shayla? Is everything alright?

I freeze, trying to think of a way to send her away and keep my dignity intact—but then I find I don't have the energy to pretend. Everything is not fine. I hobble to the door and pull it open.

Tinsdale is outside in an undershirt. It exposes the smooth

tone of her upper arms, the way their muscles link to the hard peaks of her shoulders. The lines of her collarbones are visible as well, and the curves of her figure clear beneath the fabric. I stifle the urge to pull the collar of my nightgown closer.

"Yes?"

Tinsdale frowns at me. "It sounded like something fell."

There's a definite question in her tone. "It was a snake," I say.

She is clearly trying to look around the room behind me. "Was?"

I step aside and point to the bowl on the floor, the grey stain of internal fluids spreading from the shattered remains. It looks horrible, and I'm about to apologise for disturbing her.

Tinsdale says, "That was quick of you." I look back at her and catch the ghost of a smile. It vanishes. "You didn't get bitten, did you?"

I realise that I'm standing hipshot, with my injured foot lifted off the ground. "Oh—no! I stepped on it."

"You should sit down." Tinsdale's hand is on my arm. I stiffen, and she releases her grip as if I've shocked her.

"I'm fine. I just need to clean up this mess." I take a limping step back towards it.

"That's ridiculous. You need to take care of yourself first." I start to protest, and she fixes me with a look. "Sit down. I'll be right back."

She's gone before I can say anything else. I sit down on the edge of the bed and inspect the bottom of my foot. Blood wells from a few fine lines where the edges of the snake's scales cut into my flesh. It smarts, but the cuts aren't deep. I'm lucky it was a small one, the sliding chitinous plates still developing to their adult strength. Ugh.

I *knew* I should have kept looking for weak points in

our walls and windows. How did Gerald ever survive on a spaceship? I choke back irritation and suppress the urge to get up and start inspecting wainscots again.

Tinsdale reappears with a handful of supplies from among those I brought to the sitting room—it seems amazing that was only yesterday morning. She kneels down at my feet. "Let me help."

"Um, okay." I have to stifle the urge to shy away from her reaching hand.

Tinsdale cups my heel and lifts it. Her touch is gentle, but I feel a shock at the touch of her skin against mine. Something shifts, tightens in the space below my lowest ribs. My breath catches.

"Sorry!" Tinsdale looks up at me. A line creases between her eyes. "I'll be done in a moment." She puts her free hand around my ankle, her grip a ring of heat that does nothing to calm the blood I'm sure is rising into my cheeks.

"No, it's…" It must just be that I'm unaccustomed. It's been so long since I felt any human flesh but Gerald's. It's not anything to do with Alis' bare shoulders and delicate hands. "It's fine," I mutter.

"Are you ticklish?" Her frown disappears into another of those almost-smiles. "I'll try to be quick." She dabs at the wound. I can barely feel the sting, but I still have to concentrate on not shivering the sole of my foot away, exposed as it is to her ministrations.

"There. Done." And she is. She smooths the sterile sealant over the wound and gently guides my foot back to the floor. The warmth of her hand lingers after she lets me go. A ghost sensation.

I shouldn't feel this flustered. This is…this is not how a

settler woman should be feeling. I test my weight on the foot, welcome the distraction of discomfort—although it's really not that bad, now. "Thank you, Captain Tinsdale."

"Alis," she reminds me.

"Alis," I echo, and she nods before looking back towards the mess I made. I hurry to add, "That was most helpful of you, but I can take care of...of the rest. I'll see you at breakfast."

She protests, but I insist until she disappears. I have to throw the carcass in the recycler and scrape the remains from the floor. The bowl is, unfortunately, undamaged.

*

I should be worn to exhaustion, but instead my limbs hum with a tension that almost feels like giddiness. I need work to settle and distract myself.

I decide that, since I've already dealt with refuse, I might as well take care of the hosses. It means a UV light bath before I go into their stall, but I feel as if I need to clean away more than dirt.

After that, it's almost breakfast time. I'm crossing back to the house when Tinsdale reappears.

The memory of her hand, a ghost touch on my instep, hits me with a guilty twinge, and I feel my face heat. I hope that, in the low light, she can't see my blush.

Apparently the awkward feeling is all on my side, because she just says easily, "You're up early."

I shrug. "I never got back to sleep, so I decided to take care of the livestock. I think my husband told you about the hosses?"

"Oh, of course. The herds that all this land is for, yes?"

"Well, right now there are only eight juvenile beasts. Foals? I don't know." I spread my hands, embarrassed at my ignorance.

"Babies?" The corner of Tindale's mouth quirks, but her tone is generous, as if we're sharing the joke. Her next words throw me back off balance, though. "And what are your projections about how they'll impact this ecosystem?"

"Projections?" Gerald's plan for hoss herds fully adapted to Erde wasn't his own creation. It follows a program that he purchased along with the embryo stock, a package deal that came from a Green Brigade-sanctioned trader, meant to provide seed resources for a range of frontier worlds. I try to think back, remember anything from Gerald's planning talk that matches Tinsdale's words. "I'm...I'm not sure. What do you mean?"

"New lifeforms adapt, if they are to thrive in a new biome," Tinsdale says.

I understand that, at least. "Of course. We're following a program of feed adjustments. It'll ease them into a diet of local plant stuffs as their digestion develops the ability to handle it. It's something to do with enzymes."

"Sure, but what about the adjustments going the other way?" I feel myself frown, and she clarifies. "They'll change to survive, and their survival will have ripple-out effects here, maybe ones that aren't obvious or easy to anticipate."

"How do you know?" I don't mean the words to come out confrontational. I'm genuinely curious. How does a spacer-for-hire throw out terms like 'biome' and 'ripple-out effects' with such easy familiarity?

Tinsdale hesitates. Then she says, "I used to be part of a frontier survey team."

"Really?" I blink in surprise. "Cygni?"

"Yes." Tinsdale's tone has tightened. "It wasn't a great experience."

"I'm sure not." Papa's criticisms of Cygni rise up in my memory.

"But I wasn't just there to drive groundcraft. I saw a lot about how the pieces of a world fit together."

I let her direct me away from Cygni. "What do you mean?"

"No one ships out on survey unless you have a range of different jobs. My main one was ecological analyst." She must sense my confusion, because she explains, "I looked at systems—not stars and their planets, but the webs of life they fostered. Those webs have a lot of invisible or hard-to-see strands."

I try to imagine Tinsdale striding across the terrain of some other, even stranger world, taking its measurements and rooting out its secrets. Somehow, the vision stabs me with another pang of loneliness. I try to shrug it away.

"As I said, I'm not sure about any projections. The day's starting, though. Shouldn't we get to breakfast and the plan for today's work?"

Tinsdale's lips fold, as if she wants to keep pursuing the point, but then she nods. I start to step past her, but she stops me with a hand on my arm. "Oh, one more thing. About the fieldwork."

"Yes?" Her hand transmits that same distracting heat as before.

"I know your husband meant to direct this work as we went. My crew is capable, but our formal training isn't in agriculture, precisely. Plus, we don't know the land the way you do, it's not our equipment or plan—and now we're even more shorthanded. Wouldn't it be better if you took his place in the field?"

I feel the objection in my mouth. It's what Gerald would have said, would have wanted me to say. But why? I could make another argument in terms he would accept: we shouldn't have uncertain strangers handling our groundcraft and mucking up his—our—land. Which of his desires should I ignore? I'm caught in an unexpected wave of rage. How am I still struggling to please him when he's not even here, likely not even conscious? I think of another day alone in the house.

I nod. "You're right, Captain Tinsdale. That's a better plan."

"Alis, remember?" I catch another flicker of her smile as I turn back to the house. Something in me—my ability to ignore my own visceral responses, maybe—wavers and collapses. I can't pretend away this feeling, for all it's nothing a good settler wife should feel. Admitting it to myself doesn't mean anything, though. It's not like I'll act on it.

*

I've already been out once today, but only in the dark and behind the house, focused on my path between barn and kitchen door. The view from the porch, in full daylight after breakfast, is a shock.

I stop and stare out at the strangeness before me.

The land that was cleared yesterday has changed overnight. The stumps and littered branches left by the mower's blades are still there, but the land the mowing exposed is now pierced by hundreds of little spikes. So many have sprung up that the dark earth, which showed yesterday beneath the wreckage of the felled plants, is tinted again with a recognisable yellowish green. The kudzu is already regrowing.

"Your husband warned us it was fast." That's Tinsdale—Alis—beside me.

"It is, but I didn't think—" I swallow, reframe my meaning. "I've never seen it grow back this quickly before. Gerald sealed the land the buildings sit on before he built, and we do have to trim the edges, but that's on an order of weeks, not days."

"Hmm." Alis peers under one hand, shading her eyes against the light. "And this is the first time you've cut so much back?"

"Since I've been here." My romantic imaginings had Gerald building the house himself, before he sent for me, but he must have hired other spacers, and not only to install the climate-controlled outbuildings. He told me the house, with all its imported and archaic detailing, was his gift to me, the home he'd always dreamed of. I was so overwhelmed that it took me until much later to realise it was missing any hint of my tastes or inclinations.

I turn that thought away, try instead to imagine what Gerald would want done about the problem at hand.

"The hosses are supposed to control the kudzu," I say, "That's what we're building the herds for. They're supposed eat it down, make profit off of the bounty of the land." They're Gerald's words in my mouth again. I hate them, although I can't seem to stop spitting them out. "But we only have eight baby hosses so far, not ready to eat anything growing."

Alis nods. "That's a future solution to a today problem."

She's not telling me what we should do. Of course not. The fact of Gerald's absence echoes between us as I try to think. I have a vague memory of him talking through land clearing techniques, some other time when I should have been paying more attention to his words. "We should burn it back."

"Burn it?" Luca echoes on my other side. I turn to see that he and Sono are both looking, not at me, but at Alis.

Alis' expression has closed again. "It's your project, Shayla." There's discomfort there, something she's not saying. I don't know how to ask her about it without looking even weaker. "Is that what you want?"

"Yes, it is," I tell them, chin out. I'm tired of being overwhelmed and overrun by all this life on Erde, snakes and small crawly things and fast-growing kudzu. I may not have taken to this world the way I should, the way Gerald expects, the way a true settler woman would, but I do know some things about life on a planet. Fire is a tool down here, controllable, not a sure path to explosive decompression. I can use it to control this situation.

Chapter Three

Even though I've made my decision, I can't stop the waffling inside my head. I wonder whether this is the step Gerald would have taken, then I'm irate with myself for craving his direction.

We use both groundcraft to cut a firebreak around the house and outbuildings. It's laborious work, and the heat rises as the day goes on, until the sun seems to hang at its zenith for hours and sweat runs down the sides of my face. When our two craft finally close the break at day's end, I'm beyond worn.

My skin feels as if it's reradiating heat in a way that tells me I've probably burned, despite the wide brim of my hat and my long sleeves. My back and arms ache from the work of emptying the filled craft bed over and over again. I would like to feel accomplished, proud of my work, but exhaustion is a film over everything. Even the fact that the outsider's ship is still gone, that I have no idea how Gerald is faring or whether it is a bad sign that he and Sayre have not returned.

I think I don't have the energy for more than a frisson of dull worry, but then my gut clenches when, as we trudge back into the house, Luca says, "Any word from Sayre, Captain?"

Alis grunts. "I've had no pingbacks. There's a whole lot

of planet between them and us, and I can't raise any local satellites." She looks at me. "This settlement. Are you on good terms with them?"

I answer without thinking. "Of course. We're all settlers. We'd always help each other." My breath catches on at that last, though. Gerald didn't get help from other settlers to do this work. I'd thought that he didn't ask for it. What if he asked and his request went unanswered, and that's why he brought these spacers here? What reception did he meet with, when Sayre brought him in desperate need? They must be helping him. Surely.

I realise Alis is looking at me as I hesitate in the house's shadow. The evening is almost at the point of half-dark it was when Gerald told me this crew was coming. I wonder how well she can see my expression in the dimness, how much it tells her.

She says, "With the care a full medical facility can provide, Settler Gainrad will still need time to rest and heal. It would make sense for Sayre to wait on his recovery and return with him." Her tone is even, reassuring.

I can feel myself latching onto the lifeline of reasoning she's given me. "Yes, that does make sense."

*

Gerald would never accept a cold dinner of leftovers, but that's all I have the energy to supply. At least no one complains. I'm barely conscious by the time I fall into bed, and my eyes don't crack again until morning.

It's actually another knock on my door that wakes me, and it takes heavy seconds until my brain can assign meaning to the sounds or force my ill-used body to move. The memory of the snake forces itself into my blurry consciousness, though, and I check the floor before I step onto it. There are no snakes, but the boards gleam in the light from the nearest window, the curtains' dappled shadows bleached by the intensity of the sun. I reach for the bedside timepiece, which confirms the disastrous lateness of the hour. How could I have slept through my alarm?

"I'm so sorry!" I call. "I don't know what happened! I'll be out soon!"

"Nothing to apologise for!" Alis' voice comes through the door.

I scramble across the room, try to dig out clean clothes, divest myself of my nightgown, and check the wild state of my hair all at the same time. "I'll only be a moment," I promise unrealistically, then add, "I'm sure you must be starving. Breakfast will be coming soon, I promise!" I can seem to stop shouting exculpations.

"Don't worry!" Alis calls back. Does she sound amused? I waver, hop on my cut foot, wince, and switch to the other one as I pull on my drawers. Alis adds, "Take your time."

I'm only slightly rumpled when I emerge into an empty hallway. I hear voices as I trot down the stairs, and I think at first they must be in the dining room.

I find it empty. The noise and movement originate instead in the space beyond. Were they that hungry? Shame combines with proprietary concern (what are they doing in my space?) as I approach the doorway to the kitchen and peer inside.

Alis is leaning against the far wall, while Luca stacks small boxes of food supplies that must have come out of their packs. Sono stands at my cooking surface, stirring something in one of my cookpots with one of my spoons, while steam rises around him. I suck in a breath—half guilt, half affront—but the rich, umami smell that comes with it distracts me from the protest I was going to make.

Alis' eyes smile as she takes me in, but it's Luca who speaks first, once he looks over and sees me. "Good morning!"

"I'm sorry," I begin, "I can't think how I came to oversleep. You shouldn't have had to—"

Luca cuts me off. "You needed that sleep. The strain you've been under, with your husband's injury and this work—don't pretend it's not a lot. You're part of our team, for right now at least, so we wanted to share the weight."

That idea is so generous, so unlike what I would expect from an outsider, a taker, that I'm momentarily silenced. Sono adds, "I would have asked about invading your kitchen, but we didn't want to disturb you before we had to. It was the lesser of two evils."

I find myself nodding, then nodding again when Luca asks about plates and serving utensils. I point things out helplessly, and he opens drawers and cabinets and makes appreciative noises.

"Lovely settings you have here. Everything matching and so well appointed," Luca comments. Sono serves out portions of whatever he's prepared and hands me one of my own bowls, filled with a mixture of what looks like grains and shredded vegetable I don't recognise. I take a cautious bite, still standing in the kitchen doorway. It's deliciously spicy, with flakes of something salty and proteinaceous to give it heft.

I try to think of the last time I've eaten something that I didn't prepare myself—was it really my wedding dinner? The memory of Cai and Julia smiling and passing around bulbs hits me so hard that I have to close my eyes against the homesick ache.

"Is it good?" I realise Sono is looking at me anxiously.

I swallow and nod, blink back tears. "Yes, it's delicious. Thank you."

We eat quickly, leaning against the kitchen cabinets, bowls tucked under our chins.

"There's more," Sono offers, as I fish for the last scraps in my bowl, but I wave him off. I can't wallow in this unexpected pocket of comfort. We need to get to work.

The others make appreciative noises as they finish. "Up to your usual standard," Luca says with a grin, and to me, "You're lucky. We have a prep rotation onboard the *Signs of Life*, and it would have been my turn, but Sono insisted the occasion called for his superior skills."

"And I needed to prevent you experimenting with that carcass as a food source," Sono adds.

Luca rolls his eyes, drama exaggerated. "I can't believe you took me seriously. There's no way I'd try to feed you that snake—"

I interrupt him. "What snake?"

Sono is laughing, and even Alis folds a smile away before she answers. "The two of them found another snake just outside their room when they got up this morning."

My scrap of comfort evaporates, gone with as much unexpected force as it appeared. "Another one, in the house?"

"It was just resting on that rug in the hallway," Sono says, and Luca nods agreement. The two men look unfazed. I whirl and rush from the room.

There's no sign of the snake in the downstairs hallway, nor any hint as to how it crept into the house. Stupid—I should have looked harder that first morning, or yesterday after the snake in my bedroom. I stride through the ground-floor rooms, parlour, dining room, pantry, hallway again. It's not as if the crack or gap will instantly reveal itself after all my careful hunting, but I can't seem to stop. If I can't prevent Erde from swarming past the fancy walls of this home, then all Gerald's work—all my work—might as well be for nothing. Even though I can't see it, I can feel the wide sky above the house pressing down, the swelling growth of the kudzu closing in from all sides, as if the house's walls aren't even there, as if they are just gauzy illusions, nothing that protects me from this world and its creatures.

I bowl past the boundaries of privacy and common sense— if the snake came in this way, why would they have found it outside in the hall?—and open the door to the room Sono and Luca have been using. There's little sign of their presence here, just two packs lying side-by-side at the foot of the bed, which one of them has remade with ship's discipline neatness. Sunlight through same lacy curtains that cloak the windows of Gerald's and my room creates a dappled pattern over the carpet's braided design, which catches at my eyes over and over again as I scan it. In my current frame of mind, it looks far too much like coiling snakes.

"They caught it without making a mess," Alis says.

I turn. She's followed me into the hallway. Does she think that's what I'm worried about? But why wouldn't she? I chose to live on this wild, teeming world, after all, and I've been working to keep this fragile, ornate house as crisp and picture-perfect as it was when Gerald brought me here. What hint does she have of the way this world's air overwhelms my lungs, or the way its irrepressible creatures outwit me? How could she know my closely held dissatisfaction?

I try to master the rush of my feelings. "I wasn't even thinking of that," I tell her. "I just don't like how they keep getting in."

"This house isn't a sealed environment." Alis doesn't shrug with her body, but I can hear *What did you expect?* in her tone.

I can't help but bristle, even though (maybe especially because) I've carried that frustration for so long myself. "It's not a ship in hard vacuum, either. We're not explorers of some alien world. We live here. This is—home." My tone, which had started hard as Gerald's, wavers at the last word. Home without Emil or Cai or Julia. Without the littles and their noise. Home with a wide, predatory sky and inexplicable snakes and winged monsters. With—and now without—Gerald.

"But it is an alien world, Shayla. Remember, this isn't the first I've seen."

"Oh yes," I'm still talking like a child, emotions seeping through all my attempts to seal them up again. "And you know *much* more than a foolish, sheltered settler woman."

"No, the opposite." Her response is quiet, and it snuffs out the inflated mess of my self-pity. "Each world I explored was different. Overwhelming. Complex in ways both obvious and subtle. Even though I was there on a mission dedicated to exploration and discovery, even then I never had the time to understand anything fully. There was always more. More movement, more species, more patterns and causes and effects below the surface of everything.

"So here, on this world, I can't pretend it's not alien. I can't say that I have its measure. You shouldn't either."

*

The young kudzu has expanded further overnight. Its frondy leaves are beginning to curl and spread, even obscuring the mown detritus in some places. It feels defiant, as if the kudzu is denying that Gerald and I, or Alis and her crew, could ever leave a permanent mark on this landscape. That thought makes me glance over my shoulder as I walk along the edge of the firebreak, to squash a foolish fear that the house has been overrun by curling stalks and leaves in the moments since we left it.

Of course it's still there, in all its gabled, lace-trimmed glory. My backward gaze hits on something odd, though. A thick, dark rope dangles from the porch railing. Its end grazes the ground.

No. It's not a rope. "That's the snake you caught?" My voice wavers and I have to repeat myself before the others catch all my words.

"Yes," Sono confirms. "It was curled right up outside our door. Are they cold-blooded, like Terran snakes? It was sluggish enough that I was able to grab it easily."

I swallow. "I haven't seen one that big before. You killed it with your hands?"

"Not by preference," Sono shrugs. "I'd rather not kill a specimen. But like you said, it's big enough, and we don't have the kit to be collecting live fauna samples right now."

The other two make small noises of protest, but just I stare at him, not even trying to make sense of that last bit. Sono is slighter that I am, wiry muscle on a lean frame. He seemed the quiet, retiring member of the crew, for all that he answered Luca's banter in kind at breakfast. I try to imagine him seizing a two-metre-long snake, wringing its neck…

Every time I begin to feel some kind of companionship

with these people, I'm reminded again how little I know of them, of the experiences that have shaped them and brought them here. Strangers and outsiders.

It doesn't matter. They're making good on the work they agreed to. I draw my resolution tighter than my stays and turn my back on the hanging carcass.

I've brought the little sparker from the kitchen. Flames are anathema in the fragile air bubbles of ships and stations, and it took me long enough to get used to the lamps Gerald likes to burn in the evenings. He told me that the wavering light was soft, intimate, that it complemented the design of our home, and that flammable oil was a resource we could trade for at the depot, after the glowtabs we'd brought with us ran out. It took even longer for him to convince me that we could enjoy a bonfire under the night sky from time to time.

Now I light the flame and am proud of the ease with which I hold it. I use the tool to light a fallen branch, then run it along the ragged edge of the break.

The cuttings catch first, but the fire jumps to the upswelling of new kudzu almost immediately. Little flames trace the plants' curling stems and then engulf them. White smoke billows upward until my eyes burn with it. Beneath the smoke, the fire continues to spread, the orange-red glow making the kudzu look greener in contrast, up until the moment it shrivels and blackens under the fire's heat.

I step back onto the cleared dirt, out of the reach of that heat, even as it spreads. The kudzu, for all its verdancy, burns easily, all that fast-growing energy converted into combustion. It should burn down the length of the land, away from us, away from the house and the outbuildings and all Gerald has built here. I hope the smoke stays out of the sealed barn so the hosses don't panic.

Alis, Sono and Luca spread out along the firebreak, alert for escaping sparks. I should, too.

I stand for moment, though, and watch as the smoke boils upward into the clear sky. This is my success, I tell myself. I'm keeping the work going, doing what needs to be done. I imagine myself full of possessive pride in this land, nourished by Gerald's vision, and, despite everything, I almost believe it.

*

In the groundcraft, we outpace the hungry edge of the burn. Luca is driving today, and I keep turning back to stare at the fire's progress until he grunts in surprise and the craft jerks under us.

"What?" Unnerved, I try to see in all directions at once.

"There's a lot of activity across this firebreak," Luca says. He's looking at the dirt we cleared yesterday, which stretches like a road ahead of us.

I follow his gaze and catch a flash of movement as something low and small darts out from the shadow of the low kudzu and disappears amid the press of leaves on the safe side of the break. Then there's another, a bit farther from us. And another. It's an exodus of different types of Small Things.

Ashamed of my silly names, I just say, "Those are all animals that live in and on the kudzu."

"They subsist on this stuff?" Luca's gaze flicks to the expanse of kudzu, then back to the dirt in front of us. He's slowed the groundcraft, and I can tell he's watching for more crossing creatures.

I shrug. "As far as I can tell. They do like the food we brought with us, though. I keep finding them in the house."

"If you're a new food source, I'm surprised they're not swarming in your kitchen," Luca says.

"Ugh!" I shudder at the thought. "No; it's actually less of a problem than it used to be. Only one or two every couple days—so long as we keep thing shipshape and sealed." I think of Alis' words, of my own failure to find the most recent hole.

"Maybe the population's dropping," Luca says thoughtfully.

"It doesn't look like it," I begin, pointing to where more evacuees, two of the six-legged creatures whose profiles are dominated by long, rabbit-like ears that earned their species the name Cuteish-Thing, scurry across the break ahead of us.

"Maybe—" he begins, but my hiss of indrawn breath cuts him off. Another snake coils out onto the dirt. Its arcs of chitin gleam as they slide over each other. Their movement is strange.

If I'd been in the driver's seat, I would have gunned the groundcraft and then dropped its struts onto this snake's body, but Luca just keeps on with his careful pace. The snake is gone before I can take another full breath.

"You really don't like them, do you?" Luca asks.

I force myself to shake the feeling off. "It's fine. Can you speed up a bit? We should be starting the backburn by now."

*

It's full dark and the last embers of the fires have faded to patches of smoulder. Alis and her crew have donned headlamps, and the lights move over the burnt land as they hunt lingering hot spots. My eyelids scrape every time I blink. I can't even smell smoke anymore. I want to put my head down on the steering yoke of the groundcraft.

One of the lamps bobs towards me. I squint against its one-eyed glare until I can make out Alis on foot, shovel over her shoulder, in the illumination of the groundcraft's lights. Even after this heroic day, her strides are still long. My eyes follow the way her hips move before I catch myself and lift my gaze away.

Alis reaches us, throws the shovel into the hauling bed with a clatter, and pulls herself up onto my side of the craft. The driver's bench is narrow, and she has to push close to stick to the seat. I feel the length of her thigh abut mine.

Alis says. "I think we're good. There's nothing we can find that looks like it could flare up again. Especially not near the house. I would call it a night."

"I was thinking the same thing," I tell her. It's true, but I also wish I'd felt confident enough make that decision on my own. I want to look, to catch her expression, but if I turned, we'd be nose-to-nose. Instead, I stare woodenly ahead, following the glare of the groundcraft's headlight.

After a beat, Alis says, "Good." I feel her lean her torso away, contorting herself to give me space and still keep balanced on her perch. I want to tell her it's alright if she clings to me, but the words catch, weighted, beneath my breastbone. Alis murmurs into her comm, relaying the message to Sono.

I direct the groundcraft back towards the house. The buildings ahead of us are almost invisible, nothing more than shadows in front of the emergent starfield.

We skim over the debris we've created and, once Alis' comm has finished echoing, it's as if the ashy dark has pulled the sound out of the world. Luca is silent in the opposite seat. I can feel my heartbeat in the place where Alis' and my legs touch. I should move sideways, away from her. I don't.

Even when we've pulled up before the porch, the house still looks like little more than a hulking shape above us, as strange as anything in Erde's wilderness. Alis jumps down as soon as we stop.

I feel estranged, looking up at my home. I struggle to brush off the sudden surge of alienation, remind myself I know every corner and floorboard inside this building. The porch clatters just as it always does when we climb its steps and cross to the front door. The handle is familiar in my hand.

Still, when I step inside, the others behind me, and cross the foyer, I feel as if the darkness has curled, malignant, within the enclosed space. My hand hovers above the light panel. What if I touch it and we're still encased in darkness? It feels as if another alien thing has filled this space, too thick for the light to penetrate. I grit my teeth against that foolishness and put my hand on the panel.

The lights flick on immediately, and the space is warm and familiar again—smooth panelling, tinted glass, heavy-fibered rug down the length of the foyer. For once, I don't see it first as Gerald's house.

Then I register movement.

There is a big snake helix-looping through the doorway to the sitting room. Another curls in a loose pile against the wall. There are more scattered across the floor. Kudzu-coloured, chitin-scaled, their bodies shift nauseatingly across the rug's pattern. One lies almost at my feet, so close I might have stepped on a snake for the second time in as many days.

I don't shout. The breath goes out of my body and my limbs clench as my mind orders me, uselessly, to do something.

There's a clatter and a cry by the door, the singing hiss of an energy weapon discharging. I can't look. The snake at my feet starts to move, not to flee, but coiling in tighter. They can launch themselves from that position, spring movement working in their favour, mandibles extended to grasp prey. I start to crouch, to throw myself I'm not sure where. I need to act before it does.

More shouts, and something pushes me aside. I lose my balance and stagger against the wall. When I've righted myself, I realise that Alis is there, and that a stick or rod has appeared in her hand, with which she has stabbed the snake just beneath the swell of its mandible joint. No, she hasn't stabbed it; the rod has a grasping end, which she's locked around the snake's body, just behind its skull. She lifts the snake up. Then she stops, the snake's body flailing half off the ground, the length of its helix-spiral body clasping and unclasping.

I find my voice. "What are you doing? Kill it." The foyer is full of chaos. Sono is on one knee just inside the front door, Luca's big form crumpled beside him. I can't keep my eye on all the snakes at once, or tell where they are all going. Alis is the still point in the midst of all this madness. I don't understand, but I see hesitation, the effort of holding that weight aloft at a safe distance. Her eyes go from me to her crew members and back to the snake, which still struggles to break free. Her mouth tightens, then her fist clenches as well, and the claw at the end of her tool squeezes until the snake's head flops over and its body stills, relaxing from a corkscrew to a loose rope.

Alis releases the carcass with a curse. She jabs the rod at a second snake, misses, then spears another. I cast around, searching once again for a makeshift weapon. Snakes twist and cross each other on the floor, seeking escape.

I seize the first thing that comes to hand, a fluted pitcher from the tiered shelves beneath the light panel—really, it's amazing how many purposeless vessels Gerald has littered through this house—and fling it at the snake nearest me. It's not nearly as effective as the polycrystal bowl was, though: the pitcher's delicate ceramic shatters explosively, and the snake jerks away. Its coils whip along the baseboard and disappear through the parlour doorway. Emptyhanded, I try to spot another coiling body, with some idea of stomping on it.

Except it seems I don't see any more living snakes. The floor, now scattered with ceramic shards and the dirt we've tracked in, is empty of movement. Alis stretches a second carcass next to the first she killed, and I spot another limp body at Luca and Sono's feet. I don't see any other creatures in the foyer, at least. The survivors have fled—to other parts of the house.

"Luca," Alis says, "how bad is it?" I realise that the tall man hasn't fully collapsed. Instead, he's sitting curled around one leg.

"It latched onto me." Luca's voice is shaky, and I realise with a jolt that the fabric of his pantleg above the top of his boot shows a pattern of regular perforations. Even with the dark colour of the cloth and the day's dirt, I can recognise the stain spreading from beneath. My mind fills with images of Gerald's blood-soaked shirt, and I have to fight back nausea.

"Shayla. Shayla." Alis grips my forearm, and I realise that that she's repeating herself, even as I try to focus my thoughts on the here and now. Her grip is tight enough to bruise. "Are these creatures poisonous to humans? Is there anything that won't show up in a standard bioscan?"

I swallow and find my voice. "No, they're not toxic. Their saliva is irritating, so there'll be a bit of swelling around the wound. Makes it seem like it's infected when it's not." Gerald and I found that out through a stressful period of discovery, one time when he didn't shoot a snake fast enough. "Wound care and the regular dosage of microbial adaptors are enough to make sure it heals cleanly." Some surly impulse makes me add, "We have the resources to take care of that, at least."

Alis makes a frustrated noise, and I feel immediately ashamed of my pettiness. I brace myself for a rejoinder. Instead, she helps pull Luca up, and she and Sono support him further into the house. The parallel with the way they brought Gerald in two days ago makes my chest go tight, although it's not really the same: Luca is alert and almost able to hop-limp on his own.

"Come on, Alis," he tells her, "It's not that bad."

"Then put all your weight on me," she says. "Sono, you scan for more loose fauna."

In the sitting room, Luca drops into a chair and slaps the others' hands away. Alis turns to me. "Can you help us clear the house?"

I stiffen. "What does that mean?" Strain bleeds again into pointless anger in my voice.

I can see Alis catch herself, take a breath. Part of me recognises the effort she is putting into patience, and shame makes me want to curl in on myself. I don't want to be like this in front of her. Alis speaks gently. "The fire has driven these creatures out of the underbrush. There are surely more throughout this house. Are you able to help comb through it and catch them?"

"I can do anything that needs to be done." I wish I didn't sound mulish. I should be grateful that I have this levelheaded help.

Alis looks at me, and I suspect she sees right through my roil of anger to the fear I'm trying to push down. I hope she doesn't call it out.

She just nods, though, and shows me how to work the weapon she used on the snake. It's a retractable rod with a setting in the grip that controls the hook/claw at its end. It's not particularly deadly, really; more a tool than a weapon. "Useful for keeping things at arm's length," Alis says, then shrugs when I look at her. "Better than putting more energy burns in your carpet."

Luca hands a matching rod to Alis, and all the uninjured people spread out through the house.

I go into the parlour, searching for snakes. I refuse to give in to fear and disgust in my own home. The light reveals nothing at first, though, just the room's clutter of furnishings—delicate, curved-legged chairs and little tables too low for any useful purpose, decorative vases and still-pictures on the walls that show strange planetary landscapes. It's all beginning to show dust, too, as it's days since I've done any real housework, and now we have to turn everything upside down to root out the invaders. I begin pushing furniture aside and lifting up table skirts, although I remember the disaster area in the foyer and try to move more carefully. I skirt the room's edges, since snakes generally seek out cover like the thickness of the kudzu's growth over open space.

Snakes don't make any sounds, except for the faint rasp of their chitin scales moving over each other. I try to stay quiet enough to listen for that, but I can't hear anything besides my own breath.

There's a wide cabinet against one wall, a boxy, painted thing with glass-fronted doors that holds gold-edged plates we've never used. I step around it, eyes craning as the floorspace beyond comes into view. There's the snake.

It's coiled up, ready to attack, and even as I fumble to

extend the claw tool, it launches itself towards my face.

I shout and jerk back. My hands come up almost automatically, and I strike the snake with the extended rod. Its body glances away, and it falls, twisting and recoiling itself as it goes. I press forward, trying to make the claw work as I poke at the snake. The snake moves on the floor; I can't tell if it's positioning itself to flee or attack again. The claw scrapes on its chitin as I jab and try to catch hold. The claw closes on empty air, and the snake tightens in on itself. I work the grip one more time, stab with the tool—and I've got it. It's pinned not behind the neck, where it would be most immobilised, but half a metre lower on its body. I grab the rod with both hands, work to heft the snake up as both ends flail in and out of spiral coils. It's heavy and, with the added angular weight of the rod, plus its own length, I won't be able to get it free of the ground.

In desperation, I swing the rod, snake attached, and bash it into the wall. The snake keeps flailing, and I strike it again and again. My backswing knocks it against the cabinet, which judders and lets out a crescendo of dislodged plates. I remember the claw's tightening feature, and I squeeze the grip as I dash the thing down to the floor again. I hit it one more time before the thing goes still.

"I think you got it," Alis, behind me, says into the silence. Her tone is flat enough that I choke on the urge to giggle. I can't let it bubble free, though. I don't think I'd be able to stop, or that my laughter would be distinguishable from sobs.

I start to get better at killing the snakes, though. The next couple I find are smaller, and I'm able to catch them behind the head and crush their necks after only one or two jabs with the claw. By the time we've cleared the ground floor and are onto the upper storey, I don't get quite so breathless with adrenaline before I catch one, although the moments when I'm lifting the snake away from the floor as it flails are still horrible.

At first, we pile the carcasses on the porch, but then I think better of it and tell Sono to head back out into the smoke-scented night and dig a hole to bury them. He frowns and looks around for Alis, who's still on a sweep of the upper rooms, making sure we've caught them all. The gesture knocks something loose in me, because I snap at him, "I just told you what to do—now do it!"

He retreats without another word, and I stomp back upstairs. Furniture stands higgledy-piggledy in every room; the walls are scuffed with the signs of our battles, and dirt and violent stains mar the floors. I'm exhausted, filthy, hungry, and unsure of myself, and I have no endpoint in sight. I don't know where or how Gerald is, not really. His absence is a weight, but the idea of his return is no relief.

I go through our bedroom, from which I've already removed four snakes, and into the bathroom beyond. It's one of the few spaces to have emerged largely unscathed. I wrap my arms around myself, lean my weight against the closed door, and take several long breaths, trying to reassert something like calm.

This is my favourite room in the house, the only one whose trappings feel like luxury, not just a strange and ornate contrast to my life on the *Beyond*. It's far larger than any ship or station head I've ever been in, with gleaming tiles and mirrors made of glassy polycarbon. There's a tub you can soak your whole body in, which sounds lovely right now. In my state, though, I'd just end up swimming in my own muck. Better to take a shower, even if it has to be a water one.

I ease my weight onto my own two feet again and start to peel off my clothes. I get my shirtwaist and skirts off easily enough, drop them in a dirty pile, then scrabble open the hooks of my stays and let them fall as well. The release is like lifting into freefall. The relief buoys me the last few steps to the tub. I pull the curtain back and reach in for the tap.

There's another snake curled up in the bottom of the tub.

"Oh, for the love of—!" I'm too frustrated to be frightened anymore. I grab the catching tool and get this one almost before it starts to move. My arms sag under the weight as soon as it goes limp, though. I let the snake fall back into the tub before I sit on its curved edge. I should pull on my dirty clothes, take this dead thing downstairs, help shift all these creatures we've killed, start trying to restore some order to the house…

Instead, I let my burning eyes close and my shoulders slump, elbows on knees.

I hear the faintest sound and snap alert again, sure that more snakes are coiling out from some hiding place, but it's only the click of the door opening. Alis peers in. "Was there another? Did you get it?"

*

I stand, because I don't know what else to do. I tug at the hem of my sweat-stained chemise in a futile attempt to hide the exposed length of my legs, then cross my arms in front of me.

Alis hesitates. "I'm sorry—I didn't mean to—I keep doing this…" she starts to pull her head back, but then stops. "Are you okay?"

I try to muster a response, an order, a gesture that suggests

I am in control and know what I should be doing, but I realise suddenly that if I say anything, tears will push themselves out from behind my eyes and sobs will climb out of my throat. I suck the air of this alien place in through my nose and blink again and again. I won't give in. I won't.

Alis doesn't say anything more, at first. She might have some scorn or judgement on her face, though. I can't tell because I stare at her feet as she crosses the room. She must see the snake, but she doesn't comment on it. She collapses the claw tool she's holding down to a hand's length and secures it at her belt. She pulls off first one glove, then the other. Her delicate hands are long-fingered, the tan of their skin smooth and clean next to the grime that's marked every exposed inch of her coveralls. I should have worn gloves as well. My hands are as dirty as the rest of me, blistered and chapped from wielding a shovel. I flex my fingers around my forearms, self-conscious.

Alis says, "We've combed through this place. There are no more snakes inside, and Sono told me he shoved a crate up against a hole he found in the panelling of one of the bedrooms. With the doors closed, and the window in the downstairs head shut, there shouldn't be anything else getting in tonight."

The sobs in my throat might be laughter after all. "A window was open?" My words squeak out past them. Gravity pulls me back down to the edge of the tub, and I curl around my folded arms. "What a fool I am."

Alis sits down next to me on the hard ledge. She layers one beautiful hand over another on her knee, looks at them rather than at me. "Don't punish yourself. This life is more than willing to do that for you."

In another context, I might have bitten back at that

remark—who is she to judge the life I chose? But I feel lost right now, and her tone is comforting, not bitter or accusatory. It feels like an acknowledgement of shared truth.

The comfort deepens the rifts in my self-control, though, and more words burst through. I release my arms, throw my hands out in frustration, then let them fall, defeated. "But why are there so many of them?"

Alis still doesn't turn, doesn't look at me, but one of her hands drops and finds mine. Her palm is as warm as it was before, and I feel the same twinge along every nerve of contact. I shouldn't take comfort in this stranger's touch, not here and now, practically naked and surrounded by alien carcasses. I take a deep breath, let it out.

After another moment, Alis says, "There are more snakes here than there used to be?"

I can't keep my voice from going plaintive as a child's. "I've never seen so many snakes at one time, let alone inside!"

"Well," she says, "It makes sense that there would be a shift. The factors that kept this biome in in balance aren't there anymore."

My question had been in the spirit of a curse against a perverse and uncaring universe. An actual answer is surprising enough that I look over at her face. A beat, then something, perhaps my movement, makes her turn as well. Her face is very close. It turns out her eyes aren't black, but a dark, dark brown, framed by thick lashes. She blinks, and her throat bobs as she swallows.

Then she says, "It's ecosystem disequilibrium. Fallout from what happened to the shikra."

I'm caught between sudden self-consciousness and confusion. I push back, scooting sideways on the hard edge of the tub, my hand free of hers. I've lost the thread of this conversation somewhere along the way. "What?"

Alis grimaces with what looks like chagrin. I wonder if she's as tired as I am, her usual neutral façade crumbling at the end of the day—or am I just learning to read her better?

The silence between us lengthens, makes me think I'll get no explanation, but then she shrugs, dismissing some inner conflict. "Remember I studied environmental systems? The shikra were this biome's megafauna. Apex predators, at least until the Green Brigade started hunting them down."

I remember Gerald, angry over breakfast. "That was before we even came here, though."

Alis nods, "Yes, but once the shikra were gone, or nearly, what other things started changing? These snakes, they probably made good meals for apex carnivores. Without the shikra to thin their ranks, all of a sudden there are many more of them, maybe more than this landscape can sustain.

"You said the kudzu's growth seems faster, harder to keep back?"

I nod, thinking of the press of leaves and curling stems around us. "Yes, but how does that relate?"

"The snakes are predators too. They eat creatures that are smaller, likely many of them herbivores who live in and off of the kudzu. That population starts to go down, and you see unrestrained spread as the plantlife loses its natural predators as well. It all cascades. And that's even before you introduce another invasive species."

Her words are apocalyptic. I search their meaning for blame, for punishment, and come up resistant.

"How do you know this? Are you sure?"

Alis shrugs. "I'm not sure. I wasn't on the original team,

and I'm only getting to know the specifics of this biome, but I know the patterns.

"I also know how Cygni's surveys work. They're cursory, surface level. They sketch the shape of a world, enough to allow the people that come after them to begin to fill in the gaps. We—" I frown, unsure what she means, and she clarifies, "the teams, expected that Cygni administration would put ongoing research projects in place, work that would build on what we started. But it doesn't work that way—at least, not on the planets they sign away. And as far as I know, the Green Brigade, when they bought this one, didn't do anything more except choose the easy way to make it 'safe' for settlers like you."

"And we shouldn't want to be safe?" I hear Gerald in my protest.

"That's not what I meant." Alis makes a gesture of frustration. "I only meant—it's short-sighted. Cascades begin from actions like that."

"What will happen now?"

"Lots of things. Change prompts change prompts change, until the system reaches some new equilibrium. There are many factors, many different lifeforms, elements—temperature and pressure and chemical compositions. It needs more study, before an influx of humans change it beyond recognition."

I stand and glare down at her, full of confusion of anger and guilt. "What do you mean, change it? We're not takers, not here to rape the land or destroy it. We came so we wouldn't scrabble up against other people, so we could live in a place that was untouched, unspoiled—"

I stop before any more of Gerald's words pour out. They're still hollow, even in the heat of all I feel. They aren't mine.

Alis says, "There's no environment that simply waits to welcome an invasive species and continue unchanged. Even if you knew all the patterns and forces at work within this biome, even if you didn't bring in," her eyes sweep the room around us, "alien materials and lifeforms, it wouldn't be a passive encounter. Those don't exist." She pauses, takes a deep breath, and says, "Instead you have burnt land spreading for kilometers and dead snakes in the head."

From where I'm standing, I can see down into the bathtub, behind her upturned face. I'm so tired. I can't argue with the evidence—this mess of destruction that I'm mired in—nor can I contradict any of the points she makes about shikra and snakes, disappearing Small Things or growing kudzu.

"I need to get this thing buried with the others," I tell Alis. I know my voice is wavering, defeated. "Then we need food, and to get clean enough that we can rest for the night."

I reach down and grab my claw tool and use it to lever up the snake like a gristly pennant, before I realise that, even enraged, I'm not poised enough to march downstairs in my underthings.

"I can do that." Alis stands as well. She puts her gloves back on and reaches out with protected hands to take the carcass. I hesitate, feeling one last surge of unreasonable resentment, and she looks me in the eye. I realise that she's been careful, this whole time, to keep her gaze averted from my under-dressed state, has looked nowhere below my chin. It's an act of thoughtful care that makes me even more angry, in this moment.

"Shayla," she says, "I don't doubt you do what you must to survive."

I don't know what to say to that truth, which strikes me with the force of a shikra falling from the sky, but I let her relieve me of my burden.

Chapter Four

The next day begins slowly. Everything smells of smoke, and my limbs ache from the exertions of the last few days. Alis and Sono cross and crisscross the charred land, making sure the fires are completely gone, checking to see that the ashes are cooling. Alis says we'll need to begin turning earth to bury the burnt remains under a layer of soil. That way the ashes won't blow up into the already gritty air and the land will be able to reabsorb nutrients and be ready for fresh planting. I think about the seed caches in their stable storage crates in the barn. They are the next step in Gerald's plans—but my idea of those plans has bifurcated. I can hear them still in Gerald's voice, his visions of how we will realise the bounty of Erde's landscape. At the same time, Alis' words have given those plans a shadow shape, a trajectory that includes the hunted shikras, the explosion of snakes, and the bursting, overgrowing kudzu. What is the next step in this chain of changes? What other consequences lurk within the hulls of these new seeds that I'm supposed to push into the soil?

I try not to think about the echoes of action and reaction, the things beyond my control. I try to focus on the things that are—or should be—within it. I go from room to room within the house. I do my best scrub away the dirt and soot, the stains and shreds of chitin from the snake invasion and subsequent massacre. I throw laundry into the washer and the shards of decorative ceramics into the recycler.

I'm about to start work on the next meal, but I stop in the middle of the pantry before I can start pulling out any ingredients. The hosses.

Has it been—I think back, trying to assign memories to a timeline—two days since I checked on them? Even amid the physical labour, the fire, the intruding snakes and my disturbed sleep—how could I forget about *living things* in my care?

I rush from the house, telling myself, even as I run, *it's not that bad, the feeder is on a timer; the worst that could happen is they're sitting in a bit more of their own waste than usual…* Anxiety, and the threat of Gerald's anger and disappointment, still clutches at my guts as I unseal the door to the barn.

The space inside is too quiet. I feel sick as my ears strain for the familiar squeaking noises.

When I see the lights on the monitor panel, more flickers of amber and red than constant green, it's like a terrible *I told you so*. I want to sink down right there, hide my eyes from reality.

Instead, I force myself forward, to look through the shielding curtains.

The little hosses are all lying on their sides. Fluids stain the fibrous bedding around them, imported hay that Gerald said we could soon switch out with dried kudzu fronds. I can see their little sides heaving.

It's Gerald with his bloody head; it's the kudzu growing back faster than we can cut it; the house full of snakes and everything else I couldn't control or predict. Only this is worse, because it's something that wouldn't exist if Gerald and I hadn't brought them here. We've made suffering out of nothing.

I hesitate over the panel readings—elevated respiration and heart rates, dropoff in consumption rates from the feeder. I'm feel like I should go in, to be there with them, but I have no idea what good I could do. What will Gerald say?

I'm caught by a memory of the argument over breakfast—not Gerald's words, but Alis'. Didn't she say Luca was trained in biology? I turn on my heel.

Luca sits on the top step of the porch, leaning against one of the columns. His injured leg stretches out in front of him, and he shades his eyes with one hand as he looks out over the blackened ground.

"Luca, I…"

"What is it?" He looks up, sees my face, and starts to push himself up.

"It's our livestock—the hosses. They're sick, somehow. I don't know if it's from the smoke, or something else. I thought, maybe, you might be able to…" My words run together, pitch climbing.

"I don't really know, Shayla." His words are dubious, but he starts limping forward anyway. I duck forward to take his arm, resist the urge to pull him.

"What are the symptoms?" he asks as we stagger along.

"I'm not sure. They look like they might have vomited maybe?"

"And their diet? Do they eat flora from this biome?"

"Um, they're starting to?" I try to explain the adjustment program as we get to the barn.

Luca nods before I feel as if I've clarified anything, then gestures for me to hush. He looks in at the hosses, then at the monitor panel. Then he looks back at me. "Shut off the feeder. They don't look likely to eat any more, but we shouldn't risk it."

I duck around the corner of the stall's partition, find the control panel. This is Gerald's realm, not mine, but all I have to do is find the off-switch.

Luca, without asking me, has found the barn's UV station and has turned it on himself, standing one-legged as he runs the nozzle over his boots and coverall trousers. Then he pushes through the protective curtains and lets himself down onto the soiled straw. He starts to run his hands over one of the hosses' limp bodies. I turn away, sick with helplessness.

*

It takes a long time for Luca to emerge. I sit on the ground outside the stall and worry. Eventually, my mind loses the ability to continue painting Gerald's reactions. I find myself turning back to the question of Luca's biologist knowledge. It's too similar to what Alis said about her own experience, her work with Cygni. Were they all part of a survey team? If so, how did they get from such hard-to-secure positions, onboard the coveted leap-ships that carry Cygni crews out to newly discovered worlds, to their current situation, taking unskilled labour jobs on a settler planet?

I finally hear Luca's limping steps and look up as he pushes free of the curtains.

"They were fine a few days ago?" His frown hasn't changed.

"Yes!" I assure him. "This just came over them."

"It seems to be gastric upset. Something in their guts rejecting the local biota." He turns, looking for the feeder controls. "Put them back on the original formula, with maybe some of the imported plant stuffs. No kudzu."

I don't understand. "But we eat kudzu. We've been fine. And the weaning plan, we've been following the program—"

He shrugs. "What works for you isn't working for them. Life systems are complicated. It'll likely take more work to figure out whether they can thrive in this biome. If they can."

"But the plan—" I know I'm repeating myself.

"Shayla." Luca bends over me, speaks carefully. "This planet, these creatures, they're alien to each other. We're alien to both. The ways that living things react and change when they come in contact with each other—that can't always be anticipated. You just have to assess the results and move on. Right now, moving on means going back to the old food for these little creatures and doing a serious muck out of that stall."

*

It's evening before I'm something approaching clean again.

I could make a proper meal. I could go back to my busy pretence, my irreproachable, settler's-wife duty.

Instead, I delve into the pantry for our backup rations, the stable, low-maintenance food that Gerald said we'd moved beyond, now that we are settled, but that always makes me think of the tight quarters of the *Beyond*'s galley, of handing out easy snacks to my siblings and listening to their chatter. I think the food might feel homey to the spacers as well.

I bring it out to where Alis and Sono, ash-smeared and

sweat-soaked, have joined Luca, who is back in his resting position on the porch. I don't know if he's told them about the hosses yet, and I brace myself for the shame of that discussion. But Luca just looks at the spread of little oblongs I've laid out on a plate and gives me a smile. "Kurabar. I don't mind if I do."

Alis and Sono drink deeply from the glasses of cool tea I hand them. I ignore the two chairs where Gerald and I sat and instead join the others on the floor, folding my skirts under me.

The quiet stretches, and my thoughts fill up with the whirl of the past days, the way I tried to make them, and the way they were. "I should have called a rest each day during the hottest hours. It makes no sense to keep pushing through, just doing what I thought we should.

"It's like this house. It looks the way it does because someone thought it should, not because it's most practical or most functional."

Sono says, "Why do it this way? I can't imagine the cost and effort to import so many antique materials."

"Yes," Luca adds. "All these gimcracks and flourishes, but no automed, no real security system or anything to make your life easier. It would be one thing if you were using only what you can replicate here, to build a sustainable life, maybe even a community that functions within this ecosystem, but I don't understand the thinking."

I should be insulted, but I'm not. Instead it's as if they've lowered some gate of courteous reserve to show me the truth of their feelings. They stop talking, though, look at me as if they expect me to explode like Gerald on that first morning.

I don't feel his fervour. It's time to admit it.

"Yes, it's a dream of paradise." My tone twists on the words, turning bitter. Luca looks down at the half-eaten kurabar in his hand, and Sono squints out into the light. Only Alis keeps looking at me.

I swallow. "We've been scrabbling to make that dream work since I came here. I'm exhausted."

Silence lengthens again. Finally, Alis says, "It's what you learn as you go forward."

My face must show my confusion, because she elaborates. "You learn the things that don't work and the things that do. We're always building visions of how things are and how they will be—that's human nature. Then you run up against a result, a consequence that's different from what you expect. You learn from that and you change what you do." She smiles, and it keeps her words from stinging. "The important thing is to keep watching closely, gathering data, so you do learn."

"Gathering data?" I echo.

Luca and Sono start to speak at once. "Oh, that's—" "I think what the captain means is—" Alis speaks over them. "That's what we're here to do, really."

"It's alright," she says when they give her matching frowns. "I basically almost told her last night." To me, she adds, "I told you I was on a survey team. We're here now because we don't think the surveys are thorough enough, because Cygni gives planets like this one away too easily. Because Cygni is not doing enough to protect them."

"Not doing enough…?" I stare at her. "Did Cygni send you?"

"Hah." Luca shakes his head. "No, they fired her for complaining too much."

"Which is nothing like what happened to you, of course," Sono adds.

"We all had our own reasons for leaving Cygni," Alis cuts in before Luca can launch a retort. "And we all want to know more about how biomes like Erde's work, and how we can prevent them from destabilising."

"But…" My feelings are a tangle of confusion and fierce, renewed loneliness. It's as if, by revealing these truths, they've highlighted the distances between our lives, and I'm even more alone under the sky. "But you came here to clear land."

Some intensity surges behind Alis' eyes. "Shayla." For the first time, she sounds truly unsure of herself, as if she is feeling her way to the right words. "The Green Brigade doesn't want anyone here, unless they're a settler family like yours. No Cygni, no independent researchers, no nothing. We only found out about the shikra killings by chance. They may not understand what they are doing, or they may not care, but they haven't given enough guidance to the people they send down here. Trust me." She makes another of those abortive hand gestures, as if stifling the urge to reach out. "We only came here under false pretences because we need more data, because we need to know more."

I try to pull my thoughts together. I don't really know her, or any of them. I don't. But her words ring truer than any of Gerald's ramblings.

"Here's a bit of data I've gathered." I weigh my words, "I clearly don't know enough about this, what do you call it? Biome. It seems in the interests of anyone living here to try to understand how all the other living things interact." I give her a look. "Would you know anything about doing that?"

Her smile widens, and my stomach turns over. "We might."

*

Two days later, Alis finds me before breakfast and tells me to come with her. I had planned to join Sono for the first shift of the new, moderated work pace we'd set, helping to turn the earth to mix the burned plant matter back into the soil. Two people working in the cool mornings and evenings is definitely slower, but gives space for other labours as well. Luca has been spending time with the little hosses, who, on the readjusted diet, he says are recovering well. Alis and her crew have also begun what they call 'preliminary fieldwork'.

At first, this seems to mean gathering samples of soil and cuttings—of not just the kudzu but also the smaller, wispy undergrowth plants in their surprisingly large varieties—as well as setting up recording points and sending out bug-sized drones. Those drones will, she says, capture observations of the pollinator species, the Many-Legged Things and their various cousins, and of course the snake predators.

Alis has repeated more than once that this sort of work has no quick or easy answers. I keep repeating, too, that it's alright, that I would rather go slowly, try to understand the opaque web of living things here, before we stumble into any more unforeseen consequences.

This morning, though, her expression is different when she catches me outside the kitchen. There's something bright and electric in her expression, a suppressed excitement that I've never seen before. "Shayla, let Luca take a field shift this morning. There's something I want to show you."

"What is it?" I ask, but she just flashes a smile that tugs me forward. An hour later I'm still following as she uses a forearm-length machete to cut a path beyond the edges of the cleared land.

The day has just started to warm, and the kudzu around us

rustles with unseen movement. It's the sort of noise that has always made my skin crawl, but as Alis keeps talking, sharing details about what they've found, I find myself more curious than apprehensive.

She tells me about what they've seen so far—little creatures nibbling on the lowest kudzu leaves, larger hexapods that clamber from branch to branch. I tell her about my names, and she nods, not as if they're jokes at all, and makes a note on her handheld. She describes the other snakes she's glimpsed, curled in hollows between the roots, which still makes the skin crawl around my ankles and the back of my neck. I'm glad to stay close to Alis and the swing of her machete.

I tell her that it's hard to believe her recordings already picked up so much, or that she's had a chance to review it all—does she sleep in the evenings?

She laughs, "I'm borrowing on my sleep-debt right now." Then her face sobers. "I want to get as much information as I can, while I can."

She doesn't name Gerald, but I'm sure we're both considering his return, the objections he'll be likely to raise. I try, as I've been doing over and over these last days, to imagine myself arguing back at him, pointing to his scars and marshalling Alis' points, her explanations about change and adaptation within an ecosystem. My heart sinks each time I try to paint that reality.

Alis pulls me from this latest round of worry, though, when she turns from cutting away another branch and reaches out to lay gentle fingers on my arm.

I stiffen.

"Look." Her attention is focused just ahead of us, at something within leaves of one of the taller kudzu. I follow her gaze and see an ovoid bulge that looks to be pinned between two branches. I stiffen, fear of the unknown jumping beneath my breastbone, but Alis' hand is still on my arm, her voice in my ear. "I think it's close to hatching. It's a miracle that we stopped cutting and burning where we did. A few hundred metres more and we'd have knocked it down for sure."

"Hatching…?" My question hangs, incomplete, as I peer at it. The thing—egg?—is the size of my torso. Its surface is a greenish brown that echoes the shadows among the kudzu branches, but it has a silvery sheen as well. Light filters down on it, and I realise it's slightly translucent. There is a mass within. I think of the embryo hosses in their pods—and it's as if the thing somehow sensed my thought, and I see a twitch of movement. A sharp angle presses out against the iridescent surface, and the casing (shell? sac?) bends and stretches around it.

I hear myself gasp, but it's not fear this time, or not only fear. I press forward, try to make out more of the hidden shape. The surface shivers again. Something struggles within, then goes still.

"Is it a shikra?" My voice is barely above a whisper.

"I think it will be," Alis says.

As we wait for it to move again, my mind goes back to the shadow that passed me the day Alis and the others arrived, to what happened after. I try to fit the details into a pattern that makes sense.

"Could the one that fell on Gerald be a mother?" Another thought occurs to me, and I want to duck further into the shadows beneath the leaves. I glance up to the sky. "Could it be near?"

"It's not," Alis says. "It's currently over a hundred kilometres north of us. Sayre shot it with a tracking dart as it was winging away from its attack on your husband. We've been monitoring its movements."

I forget the egg for a moment and turn on her. "You let it almost kill Gerald so you could 'monitor its movements'?" My voice shakes, "What's next? Will you feed me to some monster baby so you can understand how it grows?"

"What? No!" Alis tries to raise both hands, realises she's still holding a machete, and sheaths it at her belt. "Shayla, of course we didn't want the shikra to hurt your husband."

"But you just stood there when it happened?" I can feel the sky pressing down on me, the kudzu on all sides. How many times will I have to realise I don't know her? I want to back away from Alis, but there's nowhere to go.

"No. We were caught off guard, just like he was. If we'd been ready, if we could have gotten off shots without hitting your husband as well, we would have taken them." Alis holds my gaze. "You have to believe me, Shayla. We would never choose research over human life; I would never intentionally put you in danger. You saw how many of those snakes I killed in your house." She pauses, and when I don't say anything more, she adds. "Yes, Sayre could have slaughtered the shikra instead of tagging it, but it was fleeing; we'd beaten it away. If we'd killed it, we'd never learn any more about how its presence shapes this world.

"It's the same with this egg. I brought you because I wanted you to see the potential of it—what we could still learn, the way all these things fit together, the complexities that humans can live with and around, not just what happens when they destroy them."

We stare at each other for another long moment. I don't

know what I'm about to say, but then there's a new, slight noise and Alis' eyes move past me, towards the egg, and her expression changes. I turn to look as well.

The great oval is quivering. The surface flexes, then flexes again. The thing inside is pushing against it. The branches that hold it creak. The points of tension on the surface dimple outward, grow paler under pressure from within. There is a struggle going on. One of the points stretches, strains further—and suddenly the dark line of a crack splits open, a tear in the elastic surface, and a sharp, damp beak emerges.

The new shikra pushes its head free, eyes closed and spike-feathers matted flat with amniotic fluids. Blind, it uses its beak to dig and pulls at the edges of the tear.

Alis pulls on my arm. "Come on," she hisses.

I'm transfixed. This is a monstrous alien creature, poised to grow into something that could kill me, but I'm fascinated by its birth throes. How will it look when it emerges? Can it survive on its own right away? Was the other shikra truly its mother? Did she, if it is a she, mean to stay away? "Don't you want to see how it comes out?" I whisper back.

Alis keeps pulling. "Of course, but it shouldn't see us. I wanted to show you, but I didn't realise quite how close it was to hatching. Being here, we could affect how it responds to the world in its first moments." She echoes my own thoughts: "We know so little."

I'm about to point out that we won't learn much if we leave when she holds up another of her little drones. "We'll get a record, don't worry." She perches the little drone on a protruding twig and turns to go.

The young shikra has got a taloned foreleg out, and the tear is spreading. I can't tell if it's poised to tumble to the ground, or if it will catch itself and crawl onto one of the branches. I muscle down my curiosity and follow Alis away, but my mind stays with it, wondering at the way this world's alien mysteries can turn from threat to promise without warning.

Chapter Five

We've only just reached the edge of the burned area when Alis stops, pulls her comm unit off her belt and frowns down at it.

"What is it?" We are barely out of sight of the house, and my mind turns over itself, trying to imagine what could have happened to either of the other two in the half hour since we last saw them.

Alis says, "The *Signs of Life* just came into range."

I should feel a wash of relief. And I do; the constriction of worry and uncertainty, the helplessness of not knowing what how Gerald is faring, that promises to lift away—but there is no buoyancy in its place. Instead, my response is a tangle: apprehension and disappointment alongside the relief, guilt that I should have such a mix of feelings.

"Oh," I manage. And then, as Alis continues to stare down at her comm, "How far away are they?"

She lifts the comm to her mouth without responding to my question and says into it, "Who are they and why?"

I don't understand her words, and I open my mouth, but she holds up a hand. Sayre's response flickers on the comm's solid-state screen, and Alis grimaces and says, "Copy. We'll see you in an hour. With our hands where they can see them."

She hooks the comm into her belt and says, "What happened between your husband and the other settlers?"

"What? What are you talking about?" I stare, then start after her and she turns and begins to stride back towards the house.

I have admitted to myself, on some level, that I foresaw trouble in Gerald's return—but I hadn't imagined anything like this.

I trot after Alis as I struggle to realign my memories with her news. "I…I haven't been to the compound since before the wet season. I never spoke much to anyone there, beyond the comm station manager, and he was always friendly. Gerald didn't go on his own often, either." I think of something, "Oh—there is." My voice trails off as I consider.

"Yes?" Alis doesn't break stride, but she glances over at me.

"He brought you on." She frowns, and I amend my explanation, "He hired you all, the crew of the *Signs of Life*. I would have expected him to ask other settlers—people who already live here and might work for an exchange of favours, or out of good fellowship, rather than outsiders we don't know or trust—I mean, not that I you haven't proved yourselves more than—trustworthy, given everything—"

Alis interrupts my floundering. "Go on."

"He didn't tell me why he decided to go that way. Maybe they crossed him somehow." I try to think of the last time Gerald returned from a supply run. Was it two standard-months ago? Three? The memories blur together. Maybe he was quieter than usual as I helped him unload cartons… I catch on another detail. "The last time he came back, he brought more than usual. Good stuff, too. Didn't seem like they were on bad terms then."

Alis grimaces again. "Well, they are now. Sayre says he's got some extra passengers and they've got your husband in restraints. He says they'll give us the full story when they get here."

Alis' words fill my head, a jumble that doesn't make sense—full story, in restraints—as we crest a rise. The house and its outbuildings look more out-of-place than ever, a strange outcropping, framed by the profusion of the kudzu in the background and the blackened fields spreading at its feet. Alis calls and waves to the groundcraft, where Luca and Sono pause in their work. I don't want to hear Alis relay the news again. I don't want to have to make sense of it, to find a way forward.

My breath is wheezing in my chest. I'm clutching for the resolve, the dedication to stand strong, respond, adapt, the strength that's been my exoskeleton, firm as my stays all this time. I can't grasp at it. My stays aren't a support. They're suffocating me. I can't fill my lungs. I claw at my neckline, reach inside my blouse to release the top hooks.

"Shayla?" Alis has stopped, turned around to see why I'm no longer at her heels. I keep my hands protectively over where I've all but opened the front of my blouse, but I'm still gasping, even with room to breathe.

"Hey…hey." Alis is right in front of me now, hands on my shoulders. She doesn't look scandalised or angry or anything other than that clear, calm gaze. I could stare into her eyes forever. The thought makes my breath catch all over again, and I look down at my hands. "Hey," she says again. "Breathe with me. You can breathe." I try to follow her words, sucking air in through my nose. I'm still panting, heart hammering.

Alis leans in, wraps her arms around me. They are strong,

and I can feel the shape of her body pressed against mine. My face bumps against her collarbone. She says, "We're with you. You're not alone. We'll work this out." Her ribs swell with a deep breath, and I feel mine slowing, mimicking hers.

I try to bury myself in the moment. Just the comfort of another presence. That's all it is, I tell myself.

*

That direction helps me maintain something like calm, so that I'm standing on the porch in clean clothes, hair up in a tidy knot, by the time the *Signs of Life* eases out of the sky. My appearance is a flimsy cover, a pretence that I've stayed the model settler wife in Gerald's absence. I cringe to think of what he'll say about the state of the house, which is still dishevelled in the wake of my days of fieldwork. How will he take the news of all the things we've broken? My hands clasp in front of me, so hard that I can feel my heartbeat in the grip of my right fingers against my left wrist.

Then I want to shake myself for worrying about broken plates. What about the settlers from Erdehame? I wonder if I should have taken up Gerald's rifle, but then dismiss the idea. I can't imagine any way that threats or attempts at violence would help me or Gerald. I wonder, though, if the other settlers will see the outsiders as a threat. Alis still has her sheathed machete and Luca wears his energy weapon on his belt, although Sono is unarmed, as far as I know. I shoot a glance at where they all stand, next to me, but they all have their comms, not their weapons, out.

The ship lands directly in the space we've cleared, its struts digging into the new-turned mixture of dirt and ash. It seems bigger than I remember, a looming, eyeless creature of steel and ceramic. It sits unresponsive for long enough that I'm about to ask what Sayre is saying on the comm, when the hatch cracks open. Alis and the other two start towards it.

I feel as if I'm facing another coiled snake ready to strike at me, but I force myself forward as well, down the steps and out across the open space.

A figure steps from the shadows within the hatch, a tall, broad-shouldered man with smooth brown skin and a tailored settler's vest. I recognise him, although it takes a moment to call up his name—Laird Zuhri. I recall Gerald's introductions, one of the first times he brought me to the settlement compound, his explanation that Settler Zuhri was one of the compound's charter members, a leading voice among them. Zuhri's was one of many faces that slid by me that day, but I remember he commented on the letter in my hand and smiled in sympathy when I explained about the message for my family, far away on the *Beyond*.

"You must miss them a great deal," he said, and I bobbed vigorously, before I noted Gerald's frown out of the corner of my eye and caught myself. I still cared about disappointing him.

Now, though, I take comfort in the memory of Zuhri's kind attention. Whatever has happened with Gerald, it must be a misunderstanding, something that can be resolved through explanation, reasonable exchange between fellow settlers.

Zuhri doesn't smile now, and his hand drops onto the butt of an energy weapon as he steps onto the ground. He's followed down the short ramp by five other men I recognise but can't name, all also armed. One carries a rifle, similar to the one I saw Sayre with the first day, slung over one shoulder.

Then Gerald appears in the doorway, and my forced optimism freezes and shatters.

He's standing on his own two feet, eyes open, although I can see the remains of discoloured bruising against his hairline and along one eyebrow ridge. His broken leg is encased in a supportive splint that hinges at the knee. He steps gingerly as he moves down the ramp, although the wounded leg seems to bear his weight. I can't see bandaging beneath his clothes—but his arms are immobilised, locked together at the wrists in an involuntary mirror of my own posture.

I realise I must have frozen on an indrawn breath when his gaze meets mine. I can't read his expression, but it flickers, hardens, then he calls out, "Settlers! I've told you before, my wife is not involved in this. Any deals I made—and I still maintain that I was within my rights—your persecution of me shouldn't fall on her!"

The man with the rifle reaches back. "You should have thought of that possibility before you made takers' deals!" He takes Gerald by the upper arm and pulls him forward. It's not a violent gesture, but Gerald still lurches over his bad leg. The man's grip keeps him upright, but I feel his stumble in my own core.

Another man follows Gerald out of the ship, then Sayre's bulk fills the hatch. He's unarmed, unsmiling, but steps forward easily, without any sign of injury or physical restraint. He looks directly at Alis and she gives him the barest hint of a nod. I've stopped close beside her, a handful of paces from where the newcomers stand with Gerald at the foot of the ramp, and I realise that she's filled with coiled tension as well.

Somehow, that knowledge is comforting, as if I have someone at my back, protecting me. The notion is flawed, but it gives me enough relief that I can unlock my voice from my throat.

"Settler Zuhri, what is the meaning of this? My husband suffered an accident in the field. We thought that merited aid, in the spirit of hospitality and human decency, from a community of fellow settlers. I don't understand what has happened—why are you here, and why is he shackled?" I'm proud of how stern my voice sounds, how little it wavers.

Gerald starts to speak, "Shay, they accuse me—"

The rifle-carrying man, who has shifted his grip from Gerald's arm to his shoulder, gives him another tug, and Gerald's words break off, his face twisting. I realise that the man has him by his injured side, and my poise wavers. "No! What—"

"Easy, Karl!" Zuhri speaks over us all. "The man is still healing." Then he looks back at me. "I realise, Goodwife Gainrad, that if what your husband tells us is true and you know nothing of his betrayals, then this must be a strange and shocking development. If that is the case, I am sorry to bring you the ugly truth in this way. Nevertheless, Gerald Gainrad must face the consequences of his choices."

The man next to Zuhri adds, "Of his betrayal."

"Goodwife," Zuhri says, "Were you aware that your husband receives payments from Hyun-Raum Interests in exchange for their access to certain divisions of his land?"

"That makes no sense." I look from one of them to another, trying to read an explanation for the pain and resentment in Gerald's face. "Hyun-Raum have no stake in Erde; it's a settler world."

"They shouldn't," Zuhri agrees. "If the Green Brigade had true settler values behind it, and if there weren't selfish and short-sighted actors like your husband, willing to sell out the long-term good for their own gain."

Gerald makes another noise of protest, and I can't help but flinch, afraid of what they'll do to him. Zuhri only glances over, though, and says, "Please, Settler, repeat the argument and justifications you gave to us—although, if you hid all this from your wife and helpmeet, that says a lot about how defensible you truly believe your choices to be."

Gerald stares at me, eyes as earnest as they ever were, when he promised me a future of bountiful harvests under an unmarred sky. "Shay, you have to understand. There was no way I could have ever afforded a claim the size of ours on my own—and it is massive. This world has so much to offer, and Hyun-Raum paid well for the right to prospect in just a bit of it."

"But…" I try to gather my thoughts. "The Green Brigade opened this planet for settlers, for us…"

"Huh," I hear an echo of my father in Zuhri's tone. "The Green Brigade is hardly better than a taker's organisation. They wrap themselves in the flag of the settler cause—and, yes, they helped us get here—but don't think they won't take a cut from any deal a settler might make with exploiter companies. You signed over part of your claim to Hyun-Raum in a Green Brigade office, didn't you, Settler Gainrad?"

Gerald doesn't answer Zuhri. I try to square the man I know, the visionary who waxed lyrical about virgin land, with someone who would knowingly sell some part of it away to a corporate mining operation. He speaks quietly now, "Shay, everything we have—your beautiful house, all the wood and china, everything imported and of quality. We couldn't have had that without my deal. And where is the harm? You had no cause to learn of it—nor would these others, if Hyun-Raum hadn't overplayed its hand by offering them the same."

Another of the men snorts, "The harm? You know that Hyun-Raum plans to dig into Erde's surface, open it wide and pry out anything and everything they can use. You should have thrown that offer back in their face, as we did, as any true settler would do."

Gerald is still looking at me. "It was a small concession, a pocket of land. This world is so rich, so ready to render up its goodness to us. You have to understand—I gave just a bit of that away to ensure our future."

Maybe he would have swayed me if he'd laid out his arguments when I was still in the grasp of my first infatuation, dazzled by the fact that he'd chosen me to share his dreams. Maybe I would have accepted his choices as inevitable, when his words began to wash over me, their meanings faded and stale, during the long months we lived alone. I can't swallow them now.

"It's not," I tell him and, at his frown, "This world isn't ready to render up a bountiful harvest." I search for words, a way to show that I realise more than his hypocrisy. He is wrong in his understanding of the land, wrong in his understanding of me.

Zuhri clears his throat. He doesn't take my meaning, either. "Goodwife, let me be clear. Even after we learned how Settler Gainrad sold out, we didn't aim to persecute or punish him. He has a titled claim on this land, and—to be fair—we must still rely on the Green Brigade's protection and support, for all we now know their complicity with the resource-robbers. However, we can no longer treat him as one of us, entitled to the support, fellowship, and trade-in-kind of the settler community. He came to us in need, and we treated his injuries, used medicines that we will have to replenish through off-world trade. He has behaved as a taker, so we have to deal with him as one. The cost of the care he required, of his life saved, is the title to his claim and all its territory."

Alis speaks for the first time. "And you only just happened to come to this decision when you also have access to a crewed ship with jump capacity, one that can leave this system without relying on the relay station."

Of course. The nearest station, the one through which all communication and trade funnelled down to Erde and a few other frontier worlds, is owned and operated by the Green Brigade.

Zuhri gives her a bland look. "We do see an opportunity to hire your services, should they be available. You could carry word to other settler communities, groups that might be able to challenge the Green Brigade's control of access to this system, once they know the Brigade's true priorities. And yes, we would also ask that you take this former Settler with you. Take him to any of the hub stations. Let him try to live among the cheats and the cutthroats. He doesn't belong here."

He looks back at me, calm as if he hasn't just set fire to everything I know and expect from my life. "Goodwife Gainrad. For all his lies, your husband's assertion that you knew nothing of his deals still seems to be true." It occurs to me to wonder how much of this barrage of revelations was a test, to see if I would respond with shock? My mind is scrambling in a host of different directions, but Zuhri's next words pull my focus back to him: "You are welcome, if you wish to be free of him, to make a home with us at Erdehame."

At first, I think I must have misunderstood. "You want me to stay? Without him?"

"Marriage is a bond, and we would respect your wish to cling to it, Goodwife," Zuhri says. "But he betrayed you as well as the settler ideals. You had the good fortune all settlers dream of: the chance to live the rest of your life on a new and untouched world. His failures shouldn't rob you of that."

He waits for my response. They are all waiting, these half-familiar strangers, as the words *the rest of your life* and *new and untouched world* ring in my ears. I realise I want to turn and look at Alis, to get some clue her thoughts. I can feel her attention on me even as I keep staring at Zuhri and the rest.

I take a deep breath, but before I can speak, several things happen.

First of all, Gerald lurches sideways, twisting out of the rifleman's grip and throwing his weight hard enough against the man on the other side to throw the latter off balance. Somehow, Gerald reaches out, wrists still bound together, and grabs the staggering man so that his arms are over the man's head, the metal link of the restraints pressed against the man's throat. The man bucks and grabs at Gerald's hands, trying to claw them away.

Several people shout, and Zuhri and the rest pull their sidearms. The rifleman has his weapon off his back and up to his shoulder within a breath. Gerald pulls the body of the man he's holding, so that it's a shield between him and the others, and shouts, "Captain Tinsdale! I'll pay you more than whatever they offer. Take me and my wife to the Green Brigade relay station!"

Several of Zuhri's men look back and forth between Gerald and the rest of us, and one of them swings his weapon to point at Sayre who, I realise, also has a weapon—not his rifle but another, smaller gun. He's just holding it, though, not pointing it anywhere, and he is looking straight at Alis, who has stepped forward, close to and half in front of me.

The man in Gerald's grip chokes curses, and Gerald jerks at his neck, so hard that I wince at the violence of it. "Don't come any closer!" Gerald yells at the Erdehame men.

Alis looks around as well, her posture tense as a coiled snake. Her eyes flash back to me. "Shayla," she says, voice low, "What do you want?"

All the sudden promise of violence around us, and she's still looking at me. Before she answers Zuhri's offer, Gerald's threats and bribes. That realisation catches at me, chokes my words for another moment.

"Gainrad," Zuhri says. "Don't do this. This is no way to go out."

"This is my land!" Gerald shouts. The man in his grip is going red in the face.

I don't know what the signal was, but Zuhri and his men move as one, point their weapons up towards the sky. The noise of their combined discharge leaves my ears ringing.

"That's the warning—" Zuhri starts to say, but then the man who's been covering Sayre shouts and points away to the side, across the burned landscape, towards the path Alis and I walked that morning. The standoff's tension frays and shifts as people turn in confusion.

I look as well, and see a shadowed shape lifting from the overgrowth on a far hillock. Its wings labour, sweep down almost to brush the tops of the kudzu, and its path is irregular even as it climbs upward. It's hard to see from this distance, but I can imagine its limbs are scrawnier, its head narrow, pinions newly dried from the fight to escape its egg pod.

The rifle cracks. I expect to see the shikra tumble from the sky, but it wheels again. I hear a barrage of fire from the others, and I find my voice before I can tell whether they've found their mark.

"Wait! Stop!"

The gunfire pauses, then there's a thump and more yells, and I turn back to see that Gerald has lost control of the man he was strangling, and they've fallen to the ground, grappling and rolling over and over. Two of the others are on him now, and somewhere Zuhri is yelling, "It's too far now. Don't waste your charge," and then they've pulled Gerald loose from the man, who's collapsed coughing on his own, and they're holding Gerald down and pressing a pistol to his head as he gasps curses, and I want to be that young shikra myself, to rise up into the distant sky and away from all this.

I feel a touch on my arm and blink my eyes open. Alis drops her hand, and her gaze is on the scene in front of us, not on me, but her presence is like a stronger, more breathable set of stays. I step forward, and she keeps pace with me.

I go to where Gerald lies, trapped arms beneath him, a stranger's knee in his back, and I crouch down, so I can meet his white-rimmed, upturned eye. The man holding the gun to his head lets me push its barrel away.

I tell Gerald, "You have to let it go. The land isn't ours anymore," and then, more quietly, when I can still feel his shoulder tense and trying to flex under my hand, "Please, for my sake."

Just because he lied to me, made choices for me, that doesn't mean I want him to die like this. I will still lean into the story he believes, the one where he's my saviour and protector, if that will save his life.

He goes still, and eventually they let him climb, dirty, dishevelled, and injured, to his feet.

*

The *Signs of Life* is smaller than the *Beyond*, but its quarters aren't nearly as tight as the public transports or the Green Brigade shuttle I rode to come to Erde. It probably wouldn't feel cramped at all—if I didn't have to navigate the miasma of Gerald's hurt, confusion, and anger within its confines.

"I know I failed you," he says to me again, when he finds me in the galley midshift. We all share meal duties, even Gerald, who is technically a prisoner, but I find that I come here more often than I'm required to. The habits of bustle, of feeling responsible for a kept house, are hard to break, even when I just find myself loitering in the common spaces without enough to do.

"It's not that," I tell him, also repeating myself. I can tell he still hopes to convince me to change my mind.

When we first pushed out of Erde's gravity well, and I unhooked myself from the crash restraints, told him I wasn't going to stay by his side, he didn't understand. He thought it was as a fellow settler that I couldn't forgive him. He promised he would find a way to overcome the stain of the deal with the Green Brigade, find another settler community to join, a way to start over, to be better, to follow the ideals I was brought up with.

I tried to explain: "The settler goal—the virgin land; it wasn't real. There's no such thing."

"We can find it," he promised me. "Another fresh world. Another way to build our home."

"No," I told him. I thought it would be harder. All the times I agreed, before—all the times I thought I needed him, that I had to cleave to his dreams. It turns out it wasn't harder than any other moment I did what I had to do. "I've asked Captain Tinsdale to take you to the asteroid mining reaches. I want to visit my family, and it's as good a place to find work as any. I'll give the news about the Green Brigade to my father, let him spread it among the network of settlers, but I'm not staying with them."

"Don't be a fool!" Gerald's voice rose. "Where would you go? In this takers' universe, what could you live off of? Your body?"

The accusation was like a slap, but it made me pull away, not crumble. "That's not your concern," I told him. I left him spluttering imprecations and went to tell the first crewmember I found that I wanted my own, separate bunk for the journey.

At this point, the others have seen or heard Gerald's many attempts at apologies—over meals, at the bunkroom door, whenever he can find an opportunity to speak with me. He hasn't shouted again, but I'm almost tempted to take Alis up on her offer to lock him in the passenger cabin.

I try one more time to make him understand. "I just don't want what you want anymore. I'm not sure I ever did; it was just all I'd been raised to see."

"What do you want then?" Gerald sounds exhausted, perplexed, as if I'm a puzzle that makes no sense.

I think of the first, cautious movements of the young shikra, still hidden within its egg sac. I want to see it emerge, to witness wonders like that again. I want to understand how a reign of monster birds can balance an ecosystem so that it's not overrun by snakes and aggressive plant matter. I want to study the complexities of interactions between living things, more than 'buying,' 'taking,' 'theft,' and 'harvest.' I want to learn more about those terms that Alis has begun to elaborate for to me—parasite, symbiote, equilibrium, biome. I settle for, "I'm going to go back to Erde, somehow. As a part of this crew. I'm staying with them."

That makes no sense to him. I can see that, then I see him draw the only conclusion that would, struggle to hold back anger again. "Which one of them is it?" He asks, "That little dark one? The redhead?"

"You are out of line, Gainrad." Alis' voice is a rifle shot. She's standing in the galley's aft doorway. "Your personal union with Shayla Aru was within the mores of your settler community. If she claims it's over, then, on this ship, it is. Our crew accepts only mutual compacts. She says she's on her own path now, so you have no right to the private details of her life. Don't try my forbearance in giving you the run of this ship."

She gives him a glare that would wither kudzu, and Gerald quails before it. He mumbles something about hoping I'll come to my senses, but I can't bring myself to answer, and he turns tail rather than test Alis' resolve.

In the quiet after he leaves, I wish once again that I had something to do with my hands. I rub them against the front of my stays. I've given up skirts for pants now that we're out of the gravity well, and I'm thinking about putting off the rigid bodice too, but I haven't decided yet. I do appreciate the feeling of structure, of being held, but do I need it?

"He has no right to talk to you like that," Alis says. I look up and realise that she's still incensed. "He's a fool."

I say, "I wish I could make him see, but I guess I shouldn't be surprised. There are many people who believe they can find an unspoiled paradise that will provide everything they need. Everyone I grew up with, for one." I think about the steps forward we've discussed, which seem more and more fantastical the farther into the future they stretch. Beyond just the quandary of where to deposit Gerald, the chance to visit my family, the chore of finding a buyer on an appropriate world for the little hosses and the rest of the stock (all currently held in stasis in the ship's hold), there's the question of Erde. I think about all the Green Brigade has already done there, all the settlers intend to do... "I don't see how we're going to make anyone change. What if we can't find a way back to Erde? What if it just keeps changing?"

"Well, it'll do that regardless," Alis says, deadpan.

I clap my hand over my eyes. "Settler thinking again. Unspoiled. Polluted. I'm sorry."

"Don't be. There are bad changes and good, of course. And Erde won't be the same, now that humans are part of its world. But that's not the end of its story. The Hyun-Raum operation will go nowhere, at least."

I think of Zuhri and the others' anger, and I know that's true. "I don't think the Erdehamers will want anyone else's input though, either."

"True believers," Alis agrees, "but the data we got, the picture of life on Erde, that's changed things. Sayre's sister works on the staff of one of the undersecretaries in Cygni's regulatory department. It's not a great connection, but it is a way in. If we can get some publicity on top of that—especially if we can draw on data from studies of other alien biomes— Cygni will have to listen and act. They'll want to reexamine what's going on on places like Erde, lay down more control on cowboy operations like the Green Brigade. I'm sure there'll be a way back for people like this crew to continue mapping

Erde's complexities."

I imagine standing under that wide, ceilingless sky again, feeling the urge to hunch away from the vast spaces held within a world, and the answering determination to stand tall, look into that vastness and try to understand.

"It's something I'd like to help with." She cocks her head at me and smiles. It does things to my insides again.

I take a deep breath. I can be strong in this way, too.

"Gerald wasn't completely wrong, though," I tell Alis. "But it wasn't Luca or Sono he should be suspecting of tempting me." I can feel my cheeks heat, and I don't want to look to see her reaction. "Not Sayre, either."

There's a long pause.

"Oh," Alis says. "Well then."

I wait for more of a response, but she's standing as tightly held as I ever was. Only because I'm watching so intently, I see the subtle shift of a flush suffusing up her neck across her cheekbones.

It encourages me to take a step in. Then another one. Close enough that I feel heat in my own face, my heartbeat thudding in my throat and in other places farther down.

"The thing about changes," Alis says. Her voice is breathy, "Is they prompt change and change again. You can't always know—"

"How things will cascade," I finish for her. "That's why we need to do more research."

Alis' breath catches in a laugh. We're nose to nose again.

I can't tell if she moves first, or I do. The feeling of her lips against mine is like a newborn creature opening its wings beneath an alien sun. It's an immense skyful of possibilities, which lifts me up instead of pressing me down.

Discover Luna Novella in our store:

https://www.lunapresspublishing.com/shop

Milton Keynes UK
Ingram Content Group UK Ltd.
UKHW030256220824
447180UK00004B/33

9 781915 556035